Richard Price Hallowell

The Pioneer Quakers

Richard Price Hallowell

The Pioneer Quakers

ISBN/EAN: 9783337403072

Printed in Europe, USA, Canada, Australia, Japan

Cover: Foto ©Andreas Hilbeck / pixelio.de

More available books at **www.hansebooks.com**

THE PIONEER QUAKERS.

BY

RICHARD P. HALLOWELL.

AUTHOR OF "THE QUAKER INVASION OF MASSACHUSETTS."

SECOND EDITION.

BOSTON AND NEW YORK:

HOUGHTON, MIFFLIN AND COMPANY.

The Riverside Press, Cambridge

1887.

The Riverside Press, Cambridge:
Printed by H. O. Houghton & Co.

PREFATORY NOTE.

THE following lecture was written at the request of the Saturday Morning Club of Boston, and as much of it as time would allow was read to the club in March of the current year. In its preparation I naturally made liberal use of "The Quaker Invasion of Massachusetts," a book published by me in 1883. Nevertheless, I feel justified in saying that the reader will find not only a fresh presentation of the subject, but new and interesting matter of value to the student of American history.

The period of history to which "The Invasion" is limited ends with the year 1677, when brutality in the treatment of Quakers ceased to be a prominent factor in the orthodox religion of Massachusetts. In the present work, after giving an account of the rise of Quakerism in England, I have presented in a condensed, but I trust a concise, essay, a review of its progress in the Massachusetts Colonies, from its advent down to 1724, when the Friends secured exemption from the iniquitous and oppressive tax levied for the support of the orthodox clergy.

Some of the more flagrant errors of modern writers are indicated, and the essay closes with a brief consideration of the relations that existed between the New-England and the Pennsylvania Quakers and the native Indians.

References to authorities, not already designated in " The Invasion," will be found in the foot-notes.

R. P. H.

Boston, Mass., December, 1886.

THE PIONEER QUAKERS.

O N one occasion when Charles II. granted an audience to William Penn, the courtly Quaker, in accordance with the habit of the Quakers, entered the royal presence with his hat upon his head. The king, without comment, quietly laid aside his own hat, whereupon Penn said, "Friend Charles, why dost thou remove thy hat?" Charles, whose love of humor was one of his few redeeming characteristics, responded promptly, "It is the custom of this place for one person only to remain covered."

When I began to prepare the following paper, it occurred to me that you would find it less prosaic if the severe sobriety of the subject was relieved by this and

other anecdotes, especially if they served
to illustrate some of the unique features
of Quakerism; but as our time is limited,
and condensation is imperative, I soon
found that to adopt this plan I must sacrifice information to entertainment. I de-
cided, therefore, to tax your patience
rather than appeal to your love of amuse-
ment, by confining myself to an entirely
sober and serious account of the rise, the
mission, and the reception of the Society
of Friends in Old and New England.

The term Quaker was first applied to
these people in derision. George Fox
once bade a persecuting magistrate to
"tremble at the word of the Lord,"
whereupon the godless official jeeringly
called him a Quaker.[1] The epithet thus
fastened upon Fox and his followers has
remained to this day, but it long since
ceased to be a term of reproach. The
Quakers, however, have always called

[1] Fox's *Journal*, p. 85.

themselves Friends, thus emphasizing the fraternal bond by which they believe all men should be united. For convenience, I shall use the two words — Friends and Quakers — in this lecture, as synonymous terms; and I must ask you to remember, that, when I speak of Friends, I do not mean to indicate the social relations usually suggested by the term, but simply refer to the members of a religious sect.

George Fox, the founder of the Society of Friends, was a remarkable man, of what was perhaps the most remarkable age in the history of England. He was born in 1624, the year in which Charles I. became king. He was a young cobbler, deeply absorbed in religious meditation, when Charles was executed; an active religious zealot and martyr during the *régime* of the most distinguished parliament that ever sat in England; the most uncompromising of the motley group of innovators and reformers who defied the

despotism of Cromwell; a leading champion of morality during the reign of
Charles II., when indecency was the pass-
word to good society, and, during the
same reign, the successful defender of
religious freedom when even the stout-
est hearts quailed before the diabolical
efforts of the Anglican Church to suppress
it. Charles dying, his brother succeeded
to the throne; and in spite of the bigotry
and mean spirit usually ascribed to James,
Fox and his associates, though they were
as relentless and as inflexible as ever in
their resistance to ecclesiastical tyranny,
obtained from him a substantial recognition of their demands. William and
Mary followed the deposition of James;
and under them, in 1689, Fox lived to
read the great Act of Toleration, — an act
which marks the decline, though by no
means the entire abatement, of religious
persecution in Great Britain. Having
spent **a great part of** his mortal life in

the jails of England, and the rest of it in sturdy conflict with ecclesiastical despotism and social immorality, he passed on to immortality in the year 1690, at the age of sixty-seven, — not ripe in years, as they are counted, at least by old men, but if his life is to be measured by the broader test of deeds and the rich legacy he bequeathed to succeeding generations, no one of us can compute his age.

To understand the significance of Fox's mission, and of the peculiarities, as they are termed, of the early Quakers, I must ask you to recall the history of England during the period in which he played so conspicuous a part, and to forget for a moment that we are in the free city of Boston in the year 1886, where civil liberty is regulated by enlightened law, and our political and social conditions, though they may involve the political degradation of women, and sanction the snobbery of wealth and the tyranny of absurd customs, nevertheless do give the franchise to all men who deserve it, and do discountenance not only the grosser immoralities, but all social indecency, — at least outside of the theatre and fashionable evening parties. I must ask you to forget also that we are living at a time when, and in a city where, thanks to the courage and fidelity of the Quaker martyrs whose ashes now rest under the green turf of Boston Common, we can express our own religious convictions and theological opinions, if we have any, attend the church of our preference, if there is one, or, by our absence from all churches, signify our objection to the priestly office, without fear of fines, imprisonment, or public whipping. To understand the early Friends, we must revert to the stormy years in which they lived, when England was rent by political and religious factions; when Puritanism grappled with kingcraft, and overthrew it;

when presbyter proved to be, as Milton finely said, only " old priest writ large ; " when fanaticism marked the rise of scores of religious sects ; when intolerance inspired almost every Christian pulpit, and courts of justice were swift to punish the violation of cruel laws by barbarous penalties.

George Fox was known to his neighbors, in Leicestershire, as a youth of gentle but serious deportment, thoroughly honest and upright, unflinching in the performance of duty, but too much absorbed in mental introspection to take an active interest in public affairs. He himself, apparently, had no suspicion as to the life that was before him. His parents were members of the Established Church, and accordingly he was less under the influence of the prevailing religious excitement than adherents of the dissenting faiths ; but his nature was profoundly religious, and his boyhood was spent in continuous effort to solve the relation between himself and God. Satisfied with a limited secular education, he tended a flock of sheep, or walked alone in the fields and meadows, where, without fear of interruption, he could indulge in the study of his Bible and in spiritual meditation. He soon mastered the outward contents, the letter of the Scripture, but it was only through divine answers to constant prayer that he found their hidden treasures. This life of solitude, and devotion to spiritual matters, to the exclusion of social interests, induced a degree of morbidness that at one period threatened to destroy him. He became very wretched, both in mind and body, and, in despair, sought the advice of doctors of medicine and doctors of divinity. The medical physicians, instead of advising him to quicken the circulation of his blood by returning to active life and social intercourse, applied a lancet to his arms and head, and, in their wisdom, would have drawn from him the little blood there was left in him, but it would not flow. " His body," says one of his biographers, "seemed to be dried up with grief and trouble." The clergymen, in place of telling him to pray less and play more, only aggravated his troubles by discussing theology with him. He found them, he says, "all miserable comforters." Subsequently he consulted dissenting preachers, and occasionally some of them were of service through their religious sympathy; but this was poor medicine for a morbid mind. This utter dejection of spirit culminated in a serious illness, during which, for fourteen days, he looked so much like a corpse that many of his friends supposed him to be dead. Fortunately he recovered, and, with the return of bodily health, regained his normal mental condition. His public ministrations began at about this time (1647). The preparation for service in the cause of his Divine Master, as has been noticed, differed essentially from the prescribed method. Ecclesiastical training in the theological schools was then, as it is now, believed to be necessary to fit men for the ministry; but one result of Fox's solitary meditation was the conviction "that being bred at Oxford or Cambridge was not enough to fit and qualify men to be ministers of Christ." He discovered also that the sacredness popularly ascribed to churches was a superstitious delusion. He recognized the truth of the Scripture text, "God, who made the world, dwelleth not in temples made with hands;" and he realized that the soul of man is the temple of the Lord, which should be dedicated to his service. He learned that the Divine law is written in the hearts of men, and that to read it aright we must listen to the voice of God in our own souls. This voice of God, or divine revelation, if faithfully heeded, is, he believed, an all-suffi-

cient guide in spiritual matters. He called
it the "Inward Light," and, referring to
his public mission, says, "I was commis-
sioned to turn people to that 'Inward
Light,' even that Divine Spirit which
would lead men to all truth." Herein he
announces the fundamental principle of
Quakerism, — the Inward Light of the
Quaker. Do you ask us to explain it?
We may do so when we are able to explain the Universe, the existence of God.
Until then it will remain inexplicable.
Do you ask us if we are conscious of its
power over our own souls? We affirm it
as we affirm our own existence, and you
affirm it as often as you affirm a con-
sciousness of that part of your nature
which is spiritual. What does prayer —
not beggary, but devout, silent prayer to
God — import, if not reverential commu-
nion? I appeal to each one of you to
search your own heart devoutly, and report, if you can, that though in the exter-

nal world you find constantly renewing manifestations of Divine Intelligence, your own soul has never been penetrated and illumined by it.

The radical difference between Quakers and other Christian sects in regard to inspiration lies in the fact, that, while others limit Divine revelation to the writers of the Old and New Testaments, the Quakers claim that it is the gift of Jehovah to all men who will accept it; that the soul of man always was, and continues to be, accessible to his Creator. When Friends apply the term Father to the Supreme Intelligence, they do not use it as a mere form of language convenient for the expression of an abstract thought or theological doctrine: with them, Fatherhood implies childhood; and the relation between Father and child is an active, living, loving, intense reality. With this conception of our spiritual relations in our minds, it may be less difficult for us to appreciate the Quaker protest against an ordained ministry composed of hired officials. Professors of science and literature, and doctors of human law, Quakers believe, have their legitimate place in the social compact; but dealers in religion, doctors of the higher law, usurp the prerogatives of the Divine Teacher and Lawgiver. Intellectual training alone cannot fit men to become religious teachers. The Spirit of God must illuminate their souls, and sanctify their lives. Ordination by pope, bishop, or presbyter may make popes, bishops, and clergymen; but only the Great Head of the Church universal can commission men to preach his word.

The principle of the Inward Light is the theological basis of Quakerism; and, in fact, it is the only theological doctrine necessarily involved in Quaker religion. Fox learned the Christian dogmas at his pious mother's knee; and his adherents, who were recruited from the dissenting

sects, brought with them the prevailing
orthodox belief in the divinity of Jesus
and his infallible authority. Though not
anchored by a creed, they, unlike some of
us who have inherited their love of liberty,
accepted the Christian yoke without question; but, with great unanimity, they rejected the church dogmas of original sin,
the resurrection of the body, water baptism, and the holy sabbath day. They
believed in the inspiration of the Bible,
but held that "the letter killeth; the
Spirit giveth life;" and that, to interpret
the written word, men must be inspired
by the Spirit that guided the hands of
those who wrote it. This is an all-impor-
tant reservation, for it involves the right
of private interpretation. Under God,
Jesus was their Lord and Master; and,
with unparalleled fidelity and superb self-
sacrifice, the Quakers regulated their relations to their fellow-men by his precepts
and commands.

If Jesus taught any thing, he taught the lesson of peace; if he was positive and definite in any one command, it was where he said, "I say unto you, Swear not at all:" and yet by the verdict of Christian civilization, his authority is discredited, and his injunctions are set at naught. I am aware that Christian pulpits have always been eloquent in praise of his gospel, and fervent in exhortation to rigid obedience to his laws; but, to say nothing of aggressive warfare, even in the most enlightened nations, when the liberties of the people are threatened, or an invasion is to be resisted, this lip-service is stultified by an appeal to arms. Ploughshares and pruning-hooks are manufactured into instruments of death; and, as if to complete the satire, the name of Jesus is invoked to bless the swords of military heroes.

In the matter of oaths, the repudiation of Jesus by professing Christians is, if

possible, still more emphatic. They open
their Bibles, and read, "Swear not at all;"
and again, "My brethren, above all things,
swear not, neither by heaven, nor by earth,
nor by any other oath:" and, notwith-
standing these commands, they take an
oath as often as they sit on juries, appear
on the witness-stand, or assume the duties
of public office. I know the distinction
that is made between profanity and the
judicial oath, but I have yet to read
the scriptural warrant for one more than
for the other. Aside from scriptural condemnation of it, the Quakers' objections
to the judicial oath commend themselves
to our intelligence. They say, "It is ir-
reverent, for it is presumptuous to sum-
mon the Most High on trivial occasions;
and a proper sense of his omnipresence
should deter us from invoking his holy
name on any occasion, except in acts of
devotion." It is unnecessary; for, if the
same penalties that are attached to per-

jury were attached to falsehood, affirmation would be sufficient.

"I'll take thy word for faith, not ask thine oath :
  Who shuns not to break one, will sure crack both."

Fox and his friends, in their simplicity, believed that when their Master proclaimed peace and good will, he meant that his followers should not fight; when he commanded them not to swear, he meant they should not take an oath; and when he sent forth his disciples without purse or scrip, saying, "Freely ye have received, freely give," he did not mean that they should make merchandise of the gospel. They read his command, "Be ye not called Rabbi, for one is your master, even Christ, and all ye are brethren," and innocently supposed that Rabbi, Holy Father, and Right Reverend are interchangeable terms. Such being their interpretation of the Divine commands, they would not fight, would not take the oath of allegiance, or any other oath, would not pay church-tithes, would not call any man master, and would not recognize any distinction between the clergy and the laity. Their unswerving fidelity to their conception of Christian duty was not confined to " weightier matters of the law," but extended to matters which, to superficial observers, may seem trivial and unimportant. They used the pronouns " thee " and "thou," or, rather, they refused to use the plural number, in speaking to one person, because it is contrary to the common dialect of the whole Scripture, and because the custom originated in pride and vanity. " It was," says William Penn, " first ascribed in way of flattery to proud popes and emperors, imitating the heathens' vain homage to their gods; thereby ascribing a plural honor to a single person, as if one pope had been made up of many gods, or one emperor of many men." Barclay urges with force that " Men commonly use

the singular number to beggars and to
their servants; yea, and in their prayers
to God. Thus the superior will speak to
his inferior, who yet will not bear that the
inferior so speak to him, as judging it a
kind of reproach unto him. So hath the
pride of men placed God and the beggar
in the same category. . . . Seeing, therefore, it is manifest to us that this form of
speaking to men in the plural number
doth proceed from pride, as well as that it
is in itself a lie, we . . . testify against
it by using the singular equally unto all."
For much the same reasons, they declared
that it was not lawful for Christians either
to give or to receive titles of honor, or to
remove the hat in deference to social or
official rank.

Barclay remarks, "These titles are no
part of that obedience which is due to
magistrates or superiors, neither doth the
giving them add or diminish from that
subjection we owe to them, which consists

in obeying their just and lawful commands.
. . . It lays a necessity upon Christians
most frequently to lie, because the persons
obtaining these titles, either by election or
hereditarily, may frequently be found to
have nothing really in them deserving
them, or answering to them, — as some, to
whom it is said, Your Excellency, having
nothing of excellency in them; and he
who is called Your Grace, appears to be
an enemy to grace ; and he who is called
Your Honor, is known to be base and
ignoble.   I wonder what law of man or
what patent ought to oblige me to make a
lie, in calling good evil, and evil good.   I
wonder what law of man can secure me,
in so doing, from the just judgment of
God, that will make me account for every
idle word."

To illustrate the importance attached to
titles in those days, I need only to remind
you that even the term Master, or, as we
use it, Mister, was applied only to men of

certain rank ; and, in at least one instance,
a citizen of Massachusetts Colony was
deprived of this title by the Court in
punishment for crime.

Referring to the Friends' refusal to bow
the knee, or remove the hat, in the presence of human authority or rank, Barclay
explains, " Now, kneeling, bowing, and
uncovering the head, is the alone outward
signification of our adoration towards God ;
and therefore it is not lawful to give it
unto man. He that kneeleth or prostrates
himself to man, what doth he more to God?
He that boweth and uncovereth the head
to the creature, what hath he reserved to
the Creator? . . . They accuse us herein
of rudeness and pride: though the testimony of our consciences, in the sight of
God, be a sufficient guard against such
calumnies, yet there are of us known to
be men of such education as forbear not
these things for what they call the want
of good-breeding ; and we should be very

void of reason to purchase that pride at so dear a rate. . . . Many of us have been sorely beaten and buffeted, yea, and several months imprisoned, for no other reason but because we could not so satisfy the proud, unreasonable humors of proud men as to uncover our heads, and bow our bodies."

Many other testimonies of Friends remain to be spoken of. They asserted the right of women to preach; they were opposed to capital punishment, and demanded humane treatment of prisoners; they discountenanced the theatre, which, at the time, was a corrupting social influence; they objected to music, especially when it involved a lifetime of study; and they plead for temperance, simplicity, sobriety, and moderation in all things. "Vanity and superfluity of apparel" excited their contempt when it did not enlist their pity. In support of this testimony, Barclay quotes the apostle Paul: "I will therefore . . . in like manner also, that women adorn themselves in modest apparel, with shamefacedness and sobriety; not with broidered hair, or gold, or pearls, or costly array; but (which becometh women professing godliness) with good works." To the same purpose saith Peter, "Whose adorning let it not be that outward adorning of plaiting the hair, and of wearing of gold, or of putting on of apparel." Commenting upon these texts, Barclay says, "The adorning of Christian women (of whom it is particularly spoken, I judge, because this sex is most naturally inclined to vanity . . .) ought not to be outward, nor consist in the apparel. Is it not strange that such as make the Scripture their rule, and pretend they are guided by it, should not only be so general in the use of these things which Scripture so plainly condemns, but also should attempt to justify themselves in so doing? We see how easily men are puffed up with their garments, and how proud and vain they are when adorned to their mind. Now, how far these things are below a true Christian, and how unsuitable, needs very little proof. Hereby those who love to be gaudy and superfluous in their clothes show they concern themselves little with mortification and self-denial, and that they study to beautify their bodies more than their souls, which proves they think little upon mortality, and so certainly are more nominal than real Christians."

Some, though by no means all, of these Quaker testimonies, if urged to-day, might fairly be deemed trivial; but to realize their aptitude to the superstition, vice, and follies of the seventeenth century, we have only to mark the effect they had upon the clergy, who prospered upon the superstitious reverence of the people for their office; upon Cromwell's grim troopers, who rushed upon the swords of Prince Rupert's cavaliers, shouting hosannas to the Lord of hosts; upon judges and other civil officials, who piously insisted upon the necessity and sanctity of oaths, but, to retain office, would perjure themselves upon the advent of every new administration; and, finally, upon the dissolute, licentious, and godless panderers to the vices of the court of King Charles II.

The Society of Friends was not organized until many years after Fox began to preach, and not until his converts were counted by thousands. When they did organize, it was not in the interest of a creed, but for a philanthropic purpose, — the aid of Friends who were in prison, — and, as Fox writes, "for the promotion of purity and virtue." An habitual attendance at religious meetings was the only test of membership. If a stranger appeared in their business meetings, he was required to show a certificate from other Friends who knew him, indorsing, not his soundness in doctrine, but simply his personal character. "This precaution," says Fox, "was to prevent any bad spirit that may scandalize honest men from bringing reproach upon them." Silent meditation and solemn waiting upon the Lord was the only form of worship in their religious meetings; and, unless some one was moved by the Divine Spirit to speak or to pray, the silence was unbroken until two of the elders shook each other by the hand as a signal for adjournment.

Fox gained adherents very rapidly,— some of them eager, restless spirits, ready to follow any new light, but most of them men and women of strong and sterling character. He preached in open barns, in the fields, and in the dissenting churches, where, according to the custom of the time, men were wont to address the congregation at the close of the regular service. On very rare occasions he interrupted the minister, but on many others he was invited to occupy the pulpit. Multi-

tudes flocked to hear him, and were converted. The clergy and Government became alarmed. Such daring advocacy of
principles that strike at the root of eccle-
siastic, aristocratic, and despotic power
must be crushed out. Fear and hatred
of such bold innovators caused them to
forget their own quarrels, and to unite
for the common purpose of suppressing
Quakers. Persecution was the weapon of
both Church and State, and they wielded
it with relentless vigor. The Friends
were anathematized in the pulpits, dragged
from their meeting-houses, arraigned in
the courts, whipped in the public streets,
distrained of their property, and confined
in loathsome dungeons, where many of
them died.

Denunciation, mob violence, physical
torture, legalized robbery, and prolonged
imprisonment were wasted upon these devoted people. Members of other perse-
cuted sects held their religious meetings

secretly, and either temporized with, or plotted against, the Government. The Quakers scorned plots, compromise, and concealment, and always met openly. Even the children among them assembled, and kept up their meetings, when their parents were taken to prison. They were irrepressible and unconquerable. Cromwell paid a fine tribute to their integrity and fidelity when he said, "Now I see there is a people risen that I cannot win either with gifts, honors, offices, or places; but all other sects and people I can." Baxter, an inveterate opponent of the Quakers, acknowledges their great service to the nation. He says, referring to their constancy under the cruel operation of the Conventicle Act, "Here the Quakers did greatly relieve the sober people for a time; for they were so resolute, and so gloried in their constancy and sufferings, that they assembled openly, and were dragged away to the common jail, and yet desisted not: but the rest came next day. Abundance of them died in prison, and yet they continued their assemblies still." Orme, the biographer of Baxter, seconds this tribute. He declares, "Had there been more of the same determined spirit among others, which the Friends displayed, the sufferings of all parties would sooner have come to an end. The Government must have given way, as the spirit of the country would have been effectually aroused. The conduct of the Quakers was infinitely to their honor;" and he further remarks, "The heroic and persevering conduct of the Quakers, in withstanding the interference of Government with the rights of conscience, by which they finally secured those peculiar privileges they so richly deserve to enjoy, entitles them to the veneration of all friends of civil and religious freedom."

The fanaticism of many of the English Puritans led them into frightful excesses.

St. Paul's Cathedral and Westminster
Abbey were used as stables for horses
and as shambles for butchers. Churches
were despoiled, pictures mutilated, painted
glass destroyed, and swine baptized in
fonts, according to the established ritual.
Quaker fanaticism — for these people did
not escape the national contagion — mani-
fested itself chiefly in unique methods of
bearing testimony against a hireling ministry and barbarous laws. For example,
a Friend would sometimes appear at
church or on the street, clothed in sack-
cloth and ashes, and startle the people
by his impetuous denunciation and exhortation. "Richard Sale [I quote from
Fox's "Journal"] on a lecture day was
moved to go to the steeple-house in the
time of their worship, and to carry those
persecuting priests and people a lanthorn
and candle, as a figure of their darkness,
but they cruelly abused him, and like
dark professors as they were, put him

into their prison called Little Ease, and so squeezed his body therein that not long after, he died."

Fox seldom committed any extravagance; but he refers approvingly to those who did, and defends them by maintaining that if they acted, not in their own wills, but in the will of the Lord, they were justified. When Roger Williams denounced the Quakers because two women, impelled by religious enthusiasm, and crazed by barbarous persecution, had appeared in public in a condition better adapted to the Garden of Eden than to a New-England village, Fox not only retorted by denouncing " New-England professors " of religion for " their immodest stripping of women and maidens at the whipping-post," but said further, " We own no such practice unless the Lord upon an occasion should call for it; . . . some in New England have done the same, and have gone as a sign, . . . yet

in the innocency of God's Holy Spirit;
which they rather had chosen death in
their own wills than to have gone as they
have done; . . . there is nothing of bar-
barity or immodesty in the case; . . . and
God Almighty will judge Roger Williams
for his hard speeches against them." [1]
Erratic and misguided as a few of the
Quakers undoubtedly were, their offences
against social order were exceptionally
rare. It may safely be asserted that
there is not on record a single instance
where any one of them attempted to destroy property, or to injure a human being
in life or limb; and whatever else may be
said to their discredit, their most bitter
detractors will acknowledge that they
were pre-eminently an honest and a severely moral people.

Quakerism was an outgrowth, and, as
I read history, the consummate flower,

[1] *A New England Fire Brand Quenched*, pp. 32, 184,
196, 197, 224.

of Puritanism. Other dissenting sects lopped off the dead branches of ecclesiasticism, and essayed to make the Christian pulpit wholesome and respectable. The Quakers digged down to its very roots, and exposed their rottenness. Grim-visaged war stalked over England, rousing and exciting the brutal passions of men, and carrying death and desolation into every hamlet. Amid scenes of blood and carnage the Quakers bore aloft the banner of the Prince of peace. Priests, religious sects, Parliament, Lord Protector, and kings dallied and toyed and speculated with the principle of liberty, to extend their own power, and advance their own interests. What they claimed for themselves they denied to others. The Quaker defended liberty, not as an intellectual theory, not as a matter of policy, but as his natural, inalienable right. He demanded, not toleration and privilege, but justice. He scorned to claim for himself any right that he did not freely accord to others. No man excelled him in his praise of righteous government and enlightened law, and none equalled him in denunciation and defiance of governments and laws that robbed men of their birthright. Deference to worldly rank, to his mind, was more than form and courtesy, it involved a recognition of class distinction; it implied the superiority of such as claimed it; and therefore, while he was honest and courteous toward all men, it was a matter of conscience with him to defer to none. Every man was his brother and his peer: no man could be his master. Other reformers were innovators: he was both innovator and revolutionist. He was the democrat of democrats. Let me not be misunderstood. In calling the Quakers, democrats, I use the term in its conservative, and not at all in its destructive, sense. Quakerism and anarchism were antipodal.

There were Levellers in those days as at
present, but they were ochlocrats, not
democrats; and the Quakers were careful
to repudiate them. Quaker democracy
was of a far different type. It insisted
upon the equality of all men before the
law, but emphasized still more the responsibility of all men under the law — ruler
no less than subject. With the Quakers
every right implied a corresponding obligation and duty. Value was tested by
quality rather than by quantity. When
questions involving difference of opinion
were raised in their business meetings, the
issue depended less upon numerical ma-
jorities than upon personal character, or
what Friends still call the weight of the
meeting. Arbitrary or artificial distinctions in society, as we have seen, found
no favor with these radical reformers;
but natural distinctions, or, to use Robert
Barclay's own phrase, "natural relations," resulting from a diversity of gifts,

education and opportunity, were not only recognized, but were an essential part of the Quaker polity.

Any lecture, of mine at least, on the early Friends, addressed to a Boston audience, would be incomplete if it did not recognize our deep and permanent obligation to the Quakers of the Massachusetts and Plymouth Colonies, and include a word in vindication of their character from the aspersions of popular writers.

They were the most active, if not the only, defenders of religious liberty in the earlier days of these colonies who did not yield to, or temporize with, the intolerance, bigotry, and tyranny of Endicott, Bellingham, Norton, and other colonial rulers and clergymen, whose names, nevertheless, we are taught to venerate. For reasons which I need not now consider, most historians find it convenient to cover the cruel deeds of Massachusetts Puritans with the mantle of charity; and American history resounds with praise of their intelligence, exaltation of their piety, and apology for their cruelty, instead of with deserved condemnation of their pious stupidity, and horror for their crimes.

The plea that the Quakers were invaders was set up by the colonial officials in defence of their barbarous treatment of them, and is often renewed by modern apologists. Having already published[1] a refutation of this popular but specious plea, I will not

[1] *The Quaker Invasion of Massachusetts.* From the title of this book, one writer argues that the author concedes that the Quakers "were, in a sense, invaders." (*Vide* Higginson's *Larger History of the United States,* p. 204.) Until my attention was called to this novel construction of my use of the term "*Invasion,*" I supposed that the irony implied by it was sufficiently apparent. The futility of the plea, that, by the terms of the colonial charter, the authorities were empowered to exclude any religious nonconformist whom they chose to call an invader, is thoroughly exposed by Mr. Brooks Adams in his forthcoming volume entitled *The Emancipation of Massachusetts.* Mr. Adams's book is a masterly review of the rise and fall of ecclesiastical tyranny in Massachusetts. What I have attempted to do for the pioneer Quakers, he has accomplished not only for them, but for all other religious dissentients who figure in the colonial period of our history.

examine it here. Let me observe, however, in passing, that, to realize its inadequacy, we have only to remember that four-fifths of the Friends with whom the authorities had to deal were residents of the colonies, and many of them were owners of their habitations.

Ann Austin and Mary Fisher came here in a sailing-vessel, in July, 1656. They were the first of the Quakers who honored Massachusetts with their presence. By the laws of the colony, applicable to strangers, they were entitled to the protection of the authorities: they received such protection as the wolf gives to his helpless prey. Guiltless of offence, and without even the form of a trial, they were thrust into jail, where they remained for five weeks, when they were shipped to the Barbadoes. During their imprisonment, they were not only starved, but were subject to outrage and brutality too inhuman and indecent for recital. A few days after their enforced departure, another vessel anchored in Boston Harbor, with nine Quakers on her deck. These Friends were arrested, and, the court being in session, were duly arraigned. A long and frivolous examination, mostly upon religious doctrine, followed, at the close of which, sentence of banishment was pronounced; and instructions were issued for their close confinement until the ship in which they came should be ready for sea. The master of the ship was required to give bonds in the sum of five hundred pounds for conveying them to England at his own charge. He refused, but an arbitrary imprisonment soon brought him to submission. These Friends were in jail for about eleven weeks, during which time they were treated as dangerous criminals. Thus far the action of the rulers had not even a shadow of legal sanction, but hereafter the Quakers were to be deprived of such an unanswerable defence. The first law for their suppression and the better security of religion was passed in October, while the nine Friends were still prisoners. It begins thus: "Whereas, there is a cursed sect of heretics lately risen up in the world, which are commonly called Quakers," etc. This vituperation is followed by monstrous calumny. It provides heavy penalties for ship-masters and others who may be convicted of bringing Quakers or "Quaker books or writings concerning their devilish opinions" into the colony; and it orders that Quakers coming within the jurisdiction "shall be forthwith committed to the house of correction, and at their entrance shall be severely whipped." Such was the reception of the Quakers upon their advent here. An eminent scholar and clergyman of this city, in his contribution to a work entitled "Massachusetts and its Early History," calls it a "comedy." Some of us may be pardoned for thinking that tears of shame and sorrow and sympathy are more fitting than peals of laughter when religion is defamed, law satirized, and womanhood insulted. In a more recent newspaper article,[1] this writer, in reply to a critic, briefly, but with apparent sincerity, acknowledges the inappropriateness of his ghastly levity, which, however, the Historical Society preserves for the edification of future generations.

Nicholas Upsall, a church member and freeman as far back as 1631, lacking a proper sense of humor, had endeavored to relieve the distress of Ann Austin and Mary Fisher, and finally, when the law was proclaimed in the streets of Boston and in front of the Red Lyon Inn, of which he was proprietor, remarked "that he did look at it as a sad forerunner of some heavy judgment to fall on the country." He was immediately summoned before the court, where, making further

---

[1] *Boston Daily Advertiser*, May 4, 1883.

protest against the iniquity, he was heavily
fined, and ordered to leave the colony
within thirty days. This brave old man
was the first Boston convert to Quakerism.
Whether converted by the Quakers, who
had not been allowed to converse with
any one outside of the jail, or by the zeal-
ous and pious governor and Christian
ministers who were responsible for the
law, let each one judge. At the age of
sixty, and at the beginning of the winter
season, he was driven from his home into
the wilderness; and from that day forward until his death in 1666, he was a
constant victim to the malignant piety of
Massachusetts saints. The story is too
long to be inserted here, but it ought to
be as familiar to all of us as the story
of the "Mayflower." His gravestone and
that of his wife Dorothy still stand in
Copp's - hill Burying - ground, — humble
monuments to the memory of two of Boston's noblest heroes. Near by, one may

see the grave of Cotton Mather, the great calumniator of the Quakers, and the champion of Salem Witchcraft. Let us trust that the tender, forgiving, and enlightened spirit of the Quaker has overcome the hard, hating, superstitious spirit of the churchman, and that the proximity of their graves, undisturbed for more than two centuries, may symbolize the fraternity of their immortal souls.

Social ostracism, the whipping-post, fines, imprisonment, and banishment were resorted to in vain. They proved to be productive fertilizers of the Puritan soil, into which the Quakers who still dared to beard the Puritan wolf dropped the fructifying seed. Quakerism was soon embraced by many of the colonists, and could count in its ranks leading citizens, and former members of the church. Members of some of the most prominent and influential families eventually became identified with the despised sect. Isaac Rob-

inson, son of the illustrious pastor of the
Plymouth Pilgrims, espoused their cause
so earnestly that the court, by a special
act, disfranchised him.[1] Samuel Winthrop,
son of the first resident governor, John
Winthrop, was a distinguished Quaker;
but unfortunately he removed to Antigua.[2]
William Coddington, who accompanied
Gov. Winthrop when he brought over the
charter, and who was afterwards governor
of Rhode Island, was a leading member
of the society of Friends and an able
defender of the faith.

In October, 1657, and again in May,
1658, the law was supplemented by provisions for increased penalties. In October, 1658, the death penalty was added;
and in May, 1661, it was further ordered
that Quakers, both men and women,

---

[1] *Plymouth Colony Records,* vol. iii. p. 189; also Felt's
Ecclesiastical History, pp. 241, 243; and Sprague's *Annals
of the American Pulpit,* vol. i. p. 5.

[2] Besse, vol. ii. chap. ix. p. 171; also William
Edmundson's *Journal,* p. 61.

should "be branded with the letter R on their left shoulder, . . . stripped naked from the middle upwards, and tied to a cart's tail, and whipped through the town;" and the constables of the several towns were empowered . . . "to impress carts and oxen for the execution of this order." In November, 1661, owing to the interference of King Charles, these laws were partially suspended; but in October, 1662, they were, with the omission of the death penalty, substantially renewed.

These infamous laws were sternly executed. Four Quakers were hanged on Boston Common, three had their right ears cut off, and scores of public whippings were inflicted. One man's body was literally beaten to a jelly; and, when an indignant populace demanded punishment of the inhuman jailer who committed the crime, John Norton, the leading Christian minister, defended him. Innocent women were tied to carts, and flogged upon their bare backs until the blood streamed to their feet. On one of these occasions, the Rev. Mr. Rayner, whose appetite for mirth had probably been whetted by pious prayers and fasting, could not restrain his laughter.

After the year 1665 the lash and other instruments of physical torture fell into comparative disuse; but in 1677 the whipping-post recovered its prestige, and for a brief period was once more the favorite argument for the conversion of the Quaker heretic. Public sentiment, however, compelled the authorities to abandon it; and, so far as I know, it was never again revived. It must not be inferred, however, that the Quakers obtained immunity from other modes of persecution. On the contrary, they were constantly impoverished by the confiscation of their property to satisfy the demands of Christian ministers. They were ready and willing to pay their share towards the support of civil government;[1] but no power, human or satanic, could compel them to pay church-tithes. In 1678 the Quakers presented the following remonstrance to the General Court at Plymouth: —

"We whose names are hereunder written, called Quakers in your said jurisdiction, conscientiously and in all tenderness show why we cannot give maintenance to your present established preachers.

"We suppose it's well enough known we have never been backward to contribute our assistance in our estates and persons, where we could act without scruple of conscience, nor in the particular case of the country rate, according to our just proportion and abilities, until this late contrivance of mixing your preachers' maintenance therewith, by the which we are made incapable to bear any part of what

[1] Some writers assert the contrary; e.g., T. W. Higginson in his *Young Folks' History of the United States*, p. 80.

just charge may necessarily be disbursed for the maintenance of the civil government, — a thing we could always readily do until now. And why we cannot in conscience, directly or indirectly, pay any thing to your said preachers as such, we, in true love and tenderness (not through contention or covetousness, the Lord is our witness), offer as followeth: —

"1. The ground of a settled maintenance upon preachers, either must arise from the ceremonial law of the Jews paying tithes to their priests, the Levites, or from the Pope, who first instituted the same (as we find in history) in the Christian Church, so called, in the year 786, in the time of Offa, King of Mercia, where there was a council held by two legates sent from Pope Adrian to that purpose (see Selden's 'History of Tithes'). Now, the first, your preachers say, as well as we, is ended, and therefore will not have their maintenance called tithes. The second (viz., the Pope's institution), we suppose they will also disclaim as any precedent or ground for their practice. We must, therefore, necessarily conclude they have no ground at all, which we further demonstrate as follows: —

" 2. The gospel ought to be preached freely, according to the injunction of our Lord Jesus to his disciples when he sent them forth to preach, — 'Freely ye have received, freely give' (Matt. x. 8). This is far from bargaining for so much a year, and, if it be not paid, take away food, clothes, bedding, and what not, rather than go unpaid. Doubtless those are no true shepherds who mind the fleece more than the flock. The apostles would rather work with their own hands than make the gospel burthensome or chargeable to any (1 Thess. ii. 9; Acts xx. 34; 1 Cor. iv. (12); 2 Thess. iii. 8). Now, they are otherwise minded than the apostles who would rather make their gospel burthensome than work. The apostle coveted no man's gold or silver or apparel (Acts xx. 23). What thought will true charity allow us of those who not only covet, but forcibly take away, either gold, silver, or apparel, and that where it can (not be) well spared, from families and children? The gospel is the power of God, and therefore neither to be bought nor sold. Christ Jesus invites people freely. His ministers ought not to make people pay.

" 3. Preachers are to receive maintenance but as other men; viz., when they are poor, and want it. And here we are not backward, according to our abilities, to minister to the necessities of any men. Only this ought not to be forced or compelled from any, but ought to be left to the giver's freedom.

"4. The true ministers of Christ never received any thing (if they stood in need) but from such who had been benefited by them; and, in that case, they thought it but reasonable (as, indeed, we do, if there be occasion) that those who from them had received spirituals should (if they stood in need) communicate to them their temporals (1 Cor. ix. 11; Rom. xv. 27). Now, therefore, have we been benefited by your preachers? Do we receive of their spirituals? Say they not of us, we are heretics? Let them, therefore, first convict us, and put us into a capacity of receiving some advantage from them (if they can) before they receive maintenance from us. It is related (in the book called 'Clark's Lives') of one Rothwell, a man famous in England, in his day, that a collection having been made for him in his absence, and understanding, at his return, some had given that he was persuaded had not been profited by his preaching, he returned their money again. It were well if there were more so honestly minded.

"5. We do really believe your preachers are none of the true ministers of Christ.

Now, how can it reasonably be expected from us we should maintain or contribute towards the maintenance of such a ministry as we judge not true, without guilty consciences and manifest contradiction of ourselves and principles?

"We request, for conclusion, you will please to consider whether you may not prejudice yourselves in your public interest with the king (you yourselves having your liberty but upon sufferance), if you should compel any to conform in any respect, either by giving maintenance or otherwise, to such a church government or ministry as is repugnant to the Church of England.

"We leave the whole to your serious consideration, desiring (if it may be) we may be eased in the fore-mentioned case; viz., that you will please to distinguish between the country rate and your preachers' maintenance, and that we may not be imposed upon against our consciences;

that so, under you, we may live a peace-
able and quiet life, in all godliness and
honesty; that so, the end for which you
are placed in government being truly an-
swered, in the promotion and propagation
of the common benefit, we therein may
have our share.

"Who are your true friends,

"EDWARD WANTON.
"JOSEPH COLMAN.
"NATHAEL FITSRANDAL.
"WILLIAM ALLEN."[1]

This conflict between an intolerant and
despotic Christian Church and these un-
yielding champions of religious liberty
continued until the year 1724, when it
ended in a most welcome triumph for the
Quakers. In October of the previous
year, some Quaker assessors of Dartmouth
and Tiverton, who had been imprisoned
for refusing to collect taxes for the sup-

---

[1] *The Hinckley Papers*, pp. 18-20.

port of clergymen, appealed to the English Government. Their case was argued before the King's Privy Council; and it was decreed that the taxes in question must be remitted, and the delinquent officials released. This important event has not yet received the attention it merits from any historian of whom I have knowledge.[1] It not only marks the termination of the unmerited and barbarous persecution suffered by the Quakers for nearly three-quarters of a century, but it marks, also, the collapse of the effort made by the Puritans to establish a theocracy in Massachusetts. The petition to the King is well worth the careful attention of any one who cares to know the true character of the Quakers, and to understand the spirit by which they were animated. It reads as follows: —

"A petition to the King in the cause of

[1] I take pleasure in qualifying this statement by excepting Mr. Brooks Adams. His history was not written when this lecture was first delivered.

some Friends under sufferings in New England.

" To George, King of Great Britain, &c.

" The humble petition of Thomas Richardson and Richard Partridge, on behalf of Joseph Anthony, John Sisson, John Akin, and Philip Tabor, prisoners in the common jail at New Bristol in the king's Province of Massachusetts Bay in New England, as also of their friends (called Quakers) in general, who are frequently under great sufferings for conscience' sake in that government.

" Sheweth,

" That William and Mary, late King and Queen of England, by their royal charter bearing date the 7th day of October in the third year of their reign, did for the greater ease and encouragement of their loving subjects inhabiting said province, and of such as should come to inhabit there, grant, establish and ordain that forever thereafter there should be a liberty of conscience allowed in the worship of God to all Christians (except Papists) inhabiting, or which should inhabit or be resident within, the said province, with power also to make laws for the government of the said province, and support of the same, and to impose taxes for the king's service in the defence and support of the said government, and protection and preservation of the inhabitants, and to dispose of matters and things whereby the king's subjects there might be religiously, peaceably and civilly governed, protected and defended.

" And for the better securing and maintaining the liberty of conscience thereby granted, commanded that all such laws made and published by virtue of said charter, should be made and published under the seal of said province, and should be carefully and duly observed, kept, performed and put in execution, according to the true intent and meaning of the said charter.

" That those sects of Protestants called
Presbyterians and Independents being
more numerous in the said country than
others (to whom the said charter gives equal
rights), they became makers of the laws by
their superior numbers and votes, and ministers of the privileges of the said charter,
so as in great measure to elude the same,
and disappoint all others of the king's
Protestant subjects of the good and just
ends of their transporting themselves and
families at so great hazard and charge;
one great encouragement and inducement
thereto being liberty of conscience, and
ease from priestly impositions and bur-
thens.

" That in the year 1692 they made a law
in the said province, entitled ' An Act for
the Settlement and Support of Ministers
and School-masters,' wherein it is ordained
that the inhabitants of each town within
the said province shall take due care from
time to time to be constantly provided of

an able, learned and orthodox minister or ministers of good conversation, to dispense the word of God to them, which minister or ministers shall be suitably encouraged and sufficiently supported and maintained by the inhabitants of such towns.

" That the said law was farther enforced by another made in the year 1695, reciting the like aforesaid, as also by another made in the year 1715, entitled 'An Act for Maintaining and Propagating Religion,' in which said last act the prevention of the growth of atheism, irreligion and profaneness is suggested as one great reason of its being enacted; and the power of determining who shall be ministers under the aforesaid qualifications is by the said law assumed by the general court of assembly, with the recommendation of any three of the ministers of the same sect, already in orders, and settled and supported by virtue of the said laws ; though it was not determined (as the said petitioners humbly presume) either by the said charter, or by any act of parliament in Great Britain, or by any express law of the said province, who are orthodox or who are not, or who shall judge of such qualifications in such ministers.

" And in all which said several laws no care is had or taken of religion (even in their own sense) than only to appoint ministers of their own way, and impose their maintenance upon the king's subjects, conscientiously dissenting from them, by force of which said laws, or some of them, several of the townships within the said province have had Presbyterian and Independent preachers obtruded and imposed upon them for maintenance without their consent, and which they have not deemed able, learned and orthodox, and which as such they could not hear or receive.

" That by other laws made in the year 1722 and 1723, it is ordained that the town of Dartmouth and the town of Tiverton in the said province shall be assessed for the said years the respective sums of £100 and £72, 11*s*. over and besides the common taxes for support of the government, which sums are for maintenance of such ministers.

" That the said Joseph Anthony and John Sisson were appointed assessors of the taxes for the said town of Tiverton, and the said John Akin and said Philip Tabor for the town of Dartmouth; but some of the said assessors being of the people called Quakers, and others of them also dissenting from the Presbyterians and Independents, and greatest part of the inhabitants of the said towns being also Quakers or Anabaptists, or of different sentiment in religion from Independents and Presbyterians, the said assessors duly assessed the other taxes upon the people there, relating to the support of government, to the best of their knowledge, yet they could not in conscience assess any of the inhabitants of the said towns any thing for or towards the maintenance of any ministers.

" That the said Joseph Anthony, John Sisson, John Akin and Philip Tabor (on pretence of their non-compliance with the said law) were on the 25th of the month called May, 1723, committed to the jail aforesaid, where they still continue prisoners under great sufferings and hardships both to themselves and families, and where they must remain and die, if not relieved by the king's royal clemency and favor.

" That the said people called Quakers in the said province are, and generally have been, great sufferers by the said laws, in their cattle, horses, sheep, corn and household goods, which from time to time have been taken from them by violence of the said laws for maintenance of the said ministers, who call themselves able, learned and orthodox; which said laws, and the execution and consequences thereof, are not only (as the petitioners humbly conceive) contrary to the liberty of conscience and security of religion, civil liberty, property; and the rights and privileges granted in the said charter to all the king's Protestant subjects there, eluded and made null and precarious; but opposite to the king's royal and gracious declaration, at thy happy accession to the throne, promising protection and liberty of conscience to all thy dissenting subjects, without exception to those of the said plantations.

" That after repeated applications made to the government there, for redress in the premises, and no relief hitherto obtained (the assembly always opposing whatever the governor and council were at any time disposed to do on that behalf), the king's loyal suffering and distressed subjects do now throw themselves prostrate at the steps of the throne, humbly imploring thy

royal commiseration, that it may please
the king to denounce his negative upon
the said laws, or such part or parts of
them, or any of them, as directly or con-
sequentially affect the lives, liberties,
properties, religion or consciences of the
Protestant subjects in the said province,
and their families, and the privileges
granted and intended in the said charter,
or such other relief as thy royal wisdom
and goodness may please to provide; and
in the mean time that directions may be
given that the said Joseph Anthony, John
Sisson, John Akin and Philip Tabor be
immediately released from their imprisonment, on their giving such security in such
sums as shall be thought proper, for their
being at any time or times hereafter forthcoming when required, until their case be
brought to an issue.

"And the petitioners shall pray."

The report of the action of the Privy
Council is as follows: —

" At a court at St. James', the 2d day of June, 1724.

" PRESENT,

' The King's Most Excellent Majesty.

" His Royal Highness the Prince of Wales.

" Archbishop of Canterbury.

" Lord Chancellor.

" Lord President.

" Lord Privy Seal.

" Lord Carteret.

" Mr. Vice Chamberlain.

" William Pultney, Esq.

" Lord Chamberlain.

" Duke of Roxburgh.

" Duke of Newcastle.

" Earl of Westmoreland.

" Lord Viscount Townsend.

" Lord Viscount Torrington.

" Mr. Speaker of the House of Commons.

" Upon reading this day at the board a report from the Right Honorable the Lords of the committee of council, upon the petition of Thomas Richardson and Richard Partridge, on behalf of Joseph Anthony, John Sisson, John Akin and Philip Tabor, prisoners in the common jail at New Bristol, in his majesty's province of Massachusetts Bay in New England, for not assessing the inhabitants of the towns of Dartmouth and Tiverton the additional taxes of £100 and £72, 11s. imposed upon them by an act passed there in the year 1722, by which they appear to be for the maintenance of Presbyterian ministers, who are not of their persuasion, and also in behalf of their friends called Quakers in general, who are frequently under sufferings for conscience' sake in that government. By which report it appears, their Lordships are of opinion that it may be advisable for his majesty to remit the said additional taxes, so imposed on the said two towns, and to discharge the said persons from jail.

" His majesty in council taking the said report into consideration, is graciously pleased to approve thereof, and hereby to remit the said additional taxes of £100 and £72, 11*s.* which were, by the said act, to have been assessed on the said towns of Dartmouth and Tiverton. And his majesty is hereby further pleased to order, that the said Joseph Anthony, John Sisson, John Akin and Philip Tabor be immediately released from their imprisonment, on account thereof, which the governor, lieutenant-governor, or commander in chief for the time being of his majesty's said province of Massachusetts Bay, and all others whom it may concern, are to take notice of, and yield obedience thereunto.

"TEMPLE STANYAN."[1]

" *Vera Copia.*"

[1] Gough's *History of the Quakers*, vol. iv. pp. 219-226.

History, as it is generally written, informs us, that through their wild excesses, and contempt for civil law and social order, the Quakers goaded the Puritan authorities into enacting and executing their inhuman laws. Dr. George E. Ellis, who is almost a voluminous writer on the subject, neutralizes his praise of them when he assures us that " they were all of them of low rank, of mean breeding, and illiterate." He says they were "intrusive, pestering, indecent, and railing disturbers," who "persisted in outrages which drove the authorities almost to frenzy," and that the "legislators were beyond measure provoked and goaded to the course which they pursued." Mary Dyer, who was hanged, is described by him as one "of the most insufferable tormentors " of Boston.

James Russell Lowell tells us, in lines inspired by reverence for martyrs, that —

" History's pages but record
One death-grapple in the darkness,

'Twixt old systems and the Word;
Truth forever on the scaffold,
Wrong forever on the throne;
Yet that scaffold sways the future,
And behind the dim unknown
Standeth God within the shadow,
Keeping watch above his own."

History's pages record the erection of a
scaffold on Boston Common, upon which
the Quakers sealed their devotion to religious liberty with their blood, but Professor Lowell, remembering this scaffold, is
unable or unwilling to free himself from
the environment of Puritan tradition, and
strikes the names of its victims from his
list of "Earth's chosen heroes," with the
contemptuous remark, that they "were
martyrs to the bee in their bonnets." His
scorn for the Quakers is born of his ignorance of their faith; for ignorance alone
could lead such an intelligent writer and
distinguished champion of liberty, to speak
of Quakerism as a "gadfly" and a "mag-

got," and to pillory some of its noblest and most heroic devotees with his witty and withering censure, all of which he does in his essay on " New England Two Centuries Ago."

Hildreth wrote in fair spirit, but, in the very limited space he devotes to the subject, finds room for an occasional error. "Honest but one-eyed Mr. Palfrey"[1] relied

[1] Whether Dr. Palfrey wrote as a blind partisan or an impartial historian may be judged from his remark that "they [the Quakers] should not have been put to death. Sooner than put them to death, it were devoutly to be wished that the annoyed dwellers in Massachusetts had opened their hospitable drawing-rooms to naked women, and suffered their ministers to ascend the pulpits by steps paved with fragments of glass bottles." — *History of New England,* ii: 485. For evidence of Dr. Palfrey's indebtedness to Dr. Ellis, see p. 7 of his Preface to the same volume.

I avail myself of this mention of broken bottles to make what appears to me to be an important correction of an error that crept into *The Invasion.* When I wrote that book, I was more than willing to give the apologists for Puritan cruelties the benefit of every indecorous act charged to the Quakers, stipulating only that the citation should be authentic. In *Massachusetts and its Early History,* p. 114, and again in *The Memorial History of Boston,* vol. i. p. 184, I found it stated by Dr. Ellis that in 1658 two Quaker women entered a church in Boston, and broke bottles in the minister's

too much upon Dr. Ellis for his information, and is therefore himself untrustwor-
thy.   Bancroft repeats the blunders of

presence, "as a sign of his emptiness."   Dr. Ellis says
he obtained his information from *New Englands Ensigne*, a Quaker tract, which he found in the British
Museum.   This tract contains an account of the sufferings of Quakers in New England in 1657 and 1658, and
was published in London in 1659.   In it Humphrey
Norton and other victims of the persecution tell their
own pitiable story.   Wishing to consult original authorities wherever possible, I made diligent search, by
advertising and otherwise, for the *Ensigne*.   My search
was unsuccessful.   The bottle incident is not mentioned by any other authority known to me; but, as
Dr. Ellis states that he "copied" his report of the
event from the British Museum volume, I admitted it
into my book without even a question, and I did this
the more readily because he gives such excellent
Quaker authority for it.   Recently, having learned
that there is a copy of the *Ensigne* in the Carter Brown
Library at Providence, I made a careful examination
of it.   I found a very full report of the visit of the
two women at the church on a lecture-day.   They
waited quietly until the minister had done speaking,
and then, upon attempting to address the audience,
were "pulled down," and carried to prison.   The
report makes no mention whatever of the bottle scene
alleged to have been copied from it, and so graphically
described by Dr. Ellis, nor is there any mention of, or
reference to, it on any other page of the tract.   Dr.
Ellis, when he wrote, probably trusted to his memory
instead of referring to his notes, and, having in mind
the act of Thomas Newhouse in 1663, inadvertently

his predecessors.[1] Less ambitious writers, such as Mr. John Fiske, Mr. H. E. Scudder, and Charles C. Coffin, do not take the trouble to acquaint themselves with the record, or, knowing it, prefer treading in the well-worn path, to combating false historical conceptions with the simple truth. I have referred elsewhere[2] to the mistakes of Messrs. Fiske and Scudder, but hitherto have not alluded to those of Mr. Coffin. The one of which I shall now speak, is at least worthy of correction.

---

ascribed it to these two women. Until proper evidence to the contrary is produced, I shall hold to the belief that the bottle act was performed but once in New England by a Quaker; and it should be added that he (Newhouse) was subsequently disowned by the Friends.

[1] "They [the Quakers] would be entitled to perpetual honor, were it not that their own extravagances occasioned the foul enactment (the death penalty), to repeal which they laid down their lives. Far from introducing religious charity, their conduct irritated the government to pass the laws of which they were the victims. But for them, the country would have been guiltless of blood." — Bancroft's *History of the United States*, vol. i. p. 458.

[2] *The Quaker Invasion of Massachusetts.*

During the year 1764, in the town of New London, Conn., some Rogerines,[1] who, though they repudiated the Friends, were sometimes called Rogerine Quakers and Quaker Baptists, entered a church and engaged in the quiet occupation of knitting, to the annoyance of the minister, while he was preaching. This event is referred to in a sketch of the early settlement of New London that appeared in Harper's Magazine for December, 1879. The magazine-writer, as I have good reason to believe, inadvertently substituted a spinning-wheel for the knitting-needle, and erroneously speaks of the performers as Quakers. Mr. Coffin, not satisfied with copying the mistakes of this writer, to whom he is indebted for the story, apparently with-

---

[1] For an account of the Rogerines, consult Caulkin's *History of New London*, chaps. xiv., xxviii. John Rogers, founder of the sect, was a Seventh-day Baptist. For an account of his controversies with the Quakers, see William Edmundson's *Journal*, pp. 95, 103, and *Life and Travels of Samuel Bownas*, pp. 135–149, 240–242.

out malice, but certainly with a culpable disregard for historical veracity, *anticipates the scene by a full century*, and places it in the list of disorderly acts chargeable to the pioneer Quakers of Massachusetts.[1]

Apparently Mr. Coffin seldom, if ever, consults early authorities; but no such excuse can be offered for the author of "As to Roger Williams." A brief notice of one charge brought against the Quakers in this work will reveal the character of the whole book. In the year 1702 John Whiting, a Quaker writer, published his book entitled "Truth and Innocency Defended against Falsehood and Envy . . . in answer to Cotton Mather, a Priest of Boston, his calumnies, Lyes and Abuses of the People called Quakers in his laste Church History of England." After refuting a particularly obscene calumny first circulated by Increase Mather, and subsequently renewed by his son Cotton, with

[1] *Old Times in the Colonies*, chap. **xv.**

qualifying comments, Whiting adds, " Our adversaries . . . rake up such dirty stories to throw at us."

In the year 1876, Henry M. Dexter, another " Priest of Boston," and a natural successor to Cotton Mather, rakes up the same dirty story, and, with Whiting's refutation in one hand, with the other copies it with all its disgusting details, and, with a misleading comment of his own, publishes it as a piece of authentic Quaker history.[1] I shall not apply epithets to Mr. Dexter or to his book, but I do recommend to this Christian clergyman a careful study of John Whiting's titlepage when he again essays to write a history of the early colonists.

Sir Robert Walpole once exclaimed, " Read me any thing but history, for history must be false!" The history of the Massachusetts Colonies, as it is usually written, goes far to sustain his indict-

[1] *As to Roger Williams*, p. 135.

ment.[1] I protest that in their eagerness to shield, and to apologize for, the founders of the State, historians confuse facts, ignore dates, and sacrifice the truth; and the protest is fully justified by the evidence already given, but one more notable illustration may serve to enforce it. One of the acts of Quaker fanaticism frequently quoted in apology for the fiendish laws that were enacted and executed from 1656 to 1662, was performed by Margaret Brewster in the year 1677. That is, Margaret Brewster, appearing upon the scene for the first time, seventeen years after Mary Dyer was hanged, is held responsible for that judicial murder. Her fanaticism in 1677 goaded John Endicott to his murderous course in 1660. This confusion of dates is sufficiently culpable, but it is made still worse by misrepresentation of the act performed by her.[2]

[1] Bryant and Gay's *Popular History of the United States* is a notable exception. Mr. Gay is not only accurate in statement, but impartial in his judgments.

[2] Dr. Ellis in *Massachusetts and its Early History*, p. 113.

The poet may without blame —

" Perchance misdate the day or year,
And group events together by his art,
That in the chronicles lie far apart; "

but of the historian we have the right to demand not only accuracy in his statement of events, but scrupulous fidelity to the chronological order of their occurrence. Any one who chooses to consult the record will find not only that the excesses justly chargeable to the Quakers are few in number, but also conclusive chronological evidence to prove that they were the direct *result*, not the cause, of persecution; that the barbarous legislation of the Puritan authorities was due to their own religious bigotry and intolerance; that the majority of the Quakers were peaceful citizens, quite as well educated as the average colonist, and, as a class, more enlightened than their neighbors. In New England as in Old England, they were the leaders of a forlorn hope and almost forsaken cause.

When history is written by an impartial hand, Endicott, Bellingham, Norton, and their associates will still be honored as the founders of a State; but Upsall, Southwick, Wharton, and other Friends, whose names are rarely mentioned by the modern historian, will be revered as the patient, noble, self-sacrificing conservators of liberty, without which the State is a mockery and a crime.

I have devoted the time allotted me mainly to a consideration of the religious aspect of Quakerism, for it was pre-eminently a religious movement; but an adequate treatment of the subject would include much more than the mere reference to its influence upon civil and political institutions, to which I must limit myself at present.

No one can appreciate fully the entire significance of Quakerism until he has studied the history of Rhode Island, New Jersey, Pennsylvania, and the biography of William Penn. These histories furnish a complete vindication of the Quakers from the aspersions and calumnies of partisan and ignorant writers. Men and women for whom England could find no room outside of her jails, a people who in Massachusetts were only ignorant, lawless disturbers of the peace, and advocates of principles destructive to social order, are found to be, a few years later, on the banks of the Delaware, useful citizens, peaceful neighbors, and enlightened legislators. Rejecting the warnings of tradition, they trusted the American Indians, and their philosophy was justified. They made a treaty with the Indians which Voltaire alleges is the only league between them and the Christians which was never sealed by an oath, and never broken.

It was reserved for Mr. Francis Parkman to attempt to tarnish the lustre of this splendid vindication of Christ's Sermon on the Mount, by assuming that,

because the tribe with whom the Quakers
had to deal continuously, had been sub-
jected by their more powerful neighbors,
the Iroquois, they were, of necessity,
peaceful and inoffensive in their relations
with white settlers, and were incapable
of inflicting injury, or seeking revenge
for wrongs, and he assures us that "had
the Quakers planted their colony on the
banks of the St. Lawrence, or among the
warlike tribes of New England, their
shaking of hands, and assurances of tender regard, would not long have availed
to save them from the visitations of the
scalping-knife."[1] This view of the subject is not sustained by any facts yet
brought forward by the historian, but, on
the contrary, he himself furnishes ample
evidence to discredit it. Curiously enough,
he overlooks the fact, that the successful
issue of the Quaker experiment in Pennsylvania depended upon the ability of

[1] *The Conspiracy of Pontiac*, vol. i. p. 81.

the colonists to maintain amicable relations with the fierce Iroquois as well as with the more placable Delawares. For over seventy years, the colony, owing to the pacific and just policy of the Quakers, was exempt from Indian troubles; but when it was no longer controlled by Quaker influence, the frontiersmen were involved in Indian wars; and this same tribe of inoffensive Delawares, located on the Susquehanna and in the Ohio Valley, proved themselves to be, by Mr. Parkman's own confession, "exasperated savages,"[1] who resisted the encroachments of the whites with almost unparalleled courage and ferocity. ·

After my first public reading of this lecture, Mr. Parkman's attention was called to this part of it; and in reply, he urged that "if the Iroquois were friendly to the Quakers, they were still more so to the Dutch and English of New York, who

[1] *Conspiracy of Pontiac,* vol. i. p. 143.

had nothing of the Quaker spirit. Policy and self-interest made them friends, not only of Pennsylvania, but of all the English colonies."[1] Policy and self-interest, it is true, inspired their friendship for the New-York colony. The English were contending with the French for supremacy in America, and the Iroquois were the bitter enemies of the French. An alliance with the settlers of New York was, therefore, natural and politic. Common hatred for a common foe was largely the basis of that alliance, but no such motive influenced their relations with the followers of Penn. The Quakers were not contending with the French, or with rival tribes of Indians: they were not contending with any one, and the Iroquois could not hope for military aid from them under any circumstances. Their friendship for Pennsylvania was not founded upon any selfish hope or fear, but was

[1] *Boston Daily Advertiser*, May 4, 1886.

based upon the confidence inspired by
the fidelity of the Quakers to Christian
principles, in their dealings with them and
with all other men.

Mr. Parkman is high authority for all
questions involving the American Indian,
and I differ from him with hesitation and
reluctance. I have had no occasion to
question his statement of events, but cannot always accept his inferences and judgments. The fact that the Iroquois, on the
lower plane of policy and self-interest,
were induced to form alliances, and to
maintain amicable relations with some
colonies not Quaker in spirit, is not, to
my mind, sufficient reason for qualifying
our tribute to the Quakers, who by purely
Christian and humane methods secured
the good will of *every* Indian tribe, near
and remote, with which they had dealing
or intercourse.

The scepticism of Mr. Parkman as to
the efficacy of Quaker methods in dealing

with Indians, when applied to "the war-like tribes of New England," is equally unwarranted. These methods were severely and successfully tested on the occasion of King Philip's War (1675–76), when at a sacrifice involving the ruin of many towns, the destruction of a large amount of property in the sparsely inhabited settlements, and the loss of one-eleventh of her militia in battle, New England sealed the doom of her native Indian. The causes that led to the war are still matters of dispute, but no one doubts that it might have been averted by the United Colonies had they, in their Indian policy, emulated the example of Rhode Island, where the Quakers were numerous, and partially controlled the government.

The New-England Quakers and Indians were fast friends, and the Quaker books of our colonial period abound in tributes to the natives. The tribes in Massachusetts befriended the banished Quakers by receiv-

ing them into their wigwams, furnishing
them with provisions, guiding them through
the woods, and by many other acts of kind-
ness and sympathy. When Nicholas Upsall was driven from his home by the white
savages of Boston, and their brothers of
Plymouth hunted him out of that colony,
he found shelter with the less barbarous
red men of the forest; and one of them
exclaimed, "What a God have the English
who deal so with one another about the
worship of their God!"[1]

It is commonly, but very erroneously,
assumed, even by some modern Friends,
that the early Quakers were uniformly
extreme non-resistants, and that, relying
solely upon the power of moral suasion,
they condemned the application of the
principle of coercion to any and all human
relations. On the contrary, they admitted
both the propriety and the necessity of a
limited resort to physical force for the

---

[1] *New England Judged*, p. 40.

maintenance of civil government. It is even alleged that in Rhode Island, in one or two instances, they yielded to outside pressure so far as to exercise military authority in a mild degree; but, however this may be, it is certain that in every colony where they had control, the laws were enforced, offenders were arrested, and criminals were punished.

In Pennsylvania, having won the friendship of the Indians with practical assurances of their just intentions, they founded a colony in which all men were allowed liberty of conscience, and full liberty, in the words of their law, "to frequent or maintain any religious worship, place or ministry . . . without interruption or molestation." The right of suffrage was extended to all who paid their fair share of taxes, and taxes could not be levied except by the representatives of the people. The industrial schools of the present day were anticipated by a provision for the practical education of children. Nearly two hundred offences were blotted from the list of crimes subject to the death-penalty by English law. Prisons were converted into reformatory schools and workhouses. The law of Primogeniture was discarded. Affirmation was substituted for the judicial oath, and false accusers were made liable to double damages.

These illustrations indicate sufficiently the enlightened and humane character of their aims and purposes. It is no exaggeration to say that they anticipated the wisest statesmanship and political sagacity of two centuries; for since the close of the seventeenth century, the only real, substantial progress made in the science of government consists in the development and application of principles formulated and carried out by the Pennsylvania Quakers.

INDEX.

—•—•—

ACT for Settlement of Ministers, 61, 62.
Act for Maintaining Religion, 62.
Act of Toleration, 8.
Adams, Brooks, 41, 58.
Adrian, Pope, 52.
Affirmation legalized, 90.
Aiken, John, 59–70.
Allen, William, signature, 57.
Anarchism, Quakerism antipodal, 38.
A New England Fire Brand Quenched, 36.
Anglican Church, 8.
Anthony, Joseph, 59–70.
Antigua, Island of, 48.
Apostolic preaching, 53, 54.
Archbishop of Canterbury, 68.
Assessors in Tiverton and Dartmouth, 57–70.
As to Roger Williams, unwarranted charges in, 77, 78.
Austin, Ann, arrival of, 42; persecution of, 45.
Atheism feared, 62.

BANCROFT'S *History*, errors, 74, 75.
Banishment, 43, 47.
Baptism rejected, 18; of swine, 34.
Barbadoes, exiles, 42.
Barclay, Robert, plural pronouns, 22; titles, 23; kneeling, 25; quoting Paul, 26; dress, 27; natural relations, 39.

91

Basis of Quakerism, 17.

Baxter, Richard, concessions, 32; biography, 33.

Bellingham, Richard, 40, 81.

Besse, *Sufferings of the Quakers*, 48.

Bishops, ordination of, 17.

Bible, 12, 18.

Boston Common, Quakers buried in, 10; scaffold, 49, 72.

Boston Daily Advertiser, 45, 85.

Bottles broken, as a sign, 73–75.

Bownas, Samuel, *Life and Travels of*, 76.

Branding of men and women, 49.

Brewster, Margaret, 79.

Bryant and Gay's *History*, 79.

CAULKIN'S *History of New London*, 76.

Charles I. crowned, 7.

Charles II., anecdote, 5; society under, 8; court vices, 29; legal interference, 49.

Charters, royal, 41, 48, 59, 61–63.

Christians, professing, 19; and Indians, 82.

Christ, ministers of, 14; master, 21. (See *Jesus.*)

Chronological order neglected, 77, 79, 80.

Churches, sacredness of, 14; weapons of persecution, 31; despoiled, 34.

Church History of England, 77.

Civil government, 50, 89.

Clark's *Lives* quoted, 55.

Class distinctions, 38.

Clergy, 22, 28, 31.

Coddington, William, 48.

Coercion, principle of, 88, 89.

Coffin, Charles Carleton, errors, 75–77.

Colman, Joseph, signature, 57.

Conscience, rights of, 33, 52, 56–70.

Connecticut, Rogerines in, 76.

Conspiracy of Pontiac, 83, 84.

Conventicle Act, 32.
Copp's Hill Burying-Ground, 46.
Cromwell, Oliver, 8, 28, 32.
Creator, 16, 25. (See *God* and *Worship*.)

DARTMOUTH case, 57-70.
Democracy, 38, 39.
Dexter, Henry M., 78. (Author of *As to Roger Williams*.)
Divine revelation, 14, 16. (See *Inward Light*.)
Dyer, Mary, 71, 79.

EDMUNDSON'S, WILLIAM, *Journal*, cited, 48, 76.
Ellis, George E., his judgment and accuracy as a historian questioned, 71, 73-75, 79.
Emancipation of Massachusetts, 41.
Endicott, John, tyranny, 40; alleged to be goaded by Quakers, 79; an honored founder, 81.
England, remarkable age of, 7; jails, 9, 82; war, 37; Friends conveyed to, 43.
English Colonies, Indian friendship for, 85.

FANATICISM in sects, 11; English Puritans, 33; Quaker, 34.
Felt's *Ecclesiastical History*, 48.
Fighting forbidden, 21.
Fisher, Mary, arrived, 42; persecution of, 45.
Fiske, John, errors, 75.
Fitsrandal, Nathael, signature, 57.
Fox, George, ridiculed, 6; founder of sect, 7; Toleration Act, 8; youth, 11; personal advice, 12, 13; meditation, 14; dogmas early learned, 17; belief, 21; ministry, 29; adherents, 30; justification of excesses, 35.
Fox's *Journal*, anecdote, 6.
Friends, title, 7; determined spirit, 33; in colonies, 42. (See *Quakers*.)

GAY'S *History*, accurate, 79.
George the First petitioned to, 59–70.
God, 18, 24, 25, 88.
Gough's *History of the Quakers*, 70.

HANDSHAKING in meeting, 30; with the Indians,
　83.
Harper's Magazine, article in, 76.
Hats not removed, 5, 25.
Higginson, T. W., histories, 41, 51.
Hildreth's *History of the United States*, 73.
Hinckley Papers, 57.
Historical Society, paper preserved, 45.
Holy Spirit, 36.　(See *Divine* and *God*.)

INDIANS, American, relations with Quakers, 82–89.
Inspiration, 18.　(See *Bible*, *God*, and *Holy Spirit*.)
Invaders, Quakers as, 41.
Inward Light, 15, 17.

JAMES II. favors the Quakers, 8.
Jehovah, gift of, 16.　(See *God*.)
Jesus Christ, divinity, 18; teachings, 19; repudiated,
　19.
Jews, law and tithes, 52.

KNITTING in church, 76.

LAW, enlightened, 38; responsibility under, 39.
Laws, 42, 44, 48, 61, 63, 89.
Lecture Day, church disturbance, 74.
Leicestershire, Fox's home, 11.
Levellers, 39.
Liberty, principle, 37; devotion to, 81; in Pennsylva-
　nia, 89.
Liberty of conscience, 59–61, 89.

Little Ease, a prison, 35.
Lowell, James Russell, historic errors, 71-73.

Massachusetts *and its Early History,* 44, 73, 79.
Massachusetts, citizen of, loss of title, 25.
Mather, Cotton, 47, 77, 78.
Mather, Increase, 77.
Membership, test of, 29.
Memorial History of Boston, 73.
Mercia, Council at, 52.
Military authority by Quakers, 89.
Milton, John, quoted, 11.
Modern Friends, historic error, 88.
Moral suasion, 88.
Music objected to, 26.

New Bristol jail, 59, 69.
New England Judged, 88.
New Englands Ensigne, 74, 75.
New England Two Centuries Ago, 73.
Newhouse, Thomas, eccentric act, 74; disowned, 75.
New Jersey, history, 81.
New London, sketch of, 76.
New-York settlers, 84, 85.
Noblemen in Privy Council, 68.
Non-resistance, 88, 89. (See *Fighting.*)
Norton, Humphrey, 74.
Norton, John, tyranny, 40; defence of jailer, 49; founder, 81.

Oaths objected to, 19-22; sanctity, 29; with Indians, 82; abolished, 90.
Offa, King, 52.
Ohio-valley Indians, 84.
Old Times in the Colonies, 77.
Ordained ministry, 17.
Original sin, 18.

Orme, biographer of Baxter, 33.
Oxen impressed, 49.

PALFREY, JOHN GORHAM, *History of New Eng-
land*, 73, 74.
Papists not free, 60.
Parkman, Francis, 82–88.
Partridge, Richard, petition, 59–70.
Paul the apostle, 26.
Pennsylvania, 81–85, 89, 90.
Penn, William, 5, 22, 82.
Persecution, weapon, 31; immunity from, 50; ended, 58.
Peter the apostle, 27, 54.
Petition to the General Court at Plymouth, 51–57; to
the King, 58–70.
Philip, King, Indian war, 87.
Plymouth, court, 51; persecution, 88.
Plymouth Colony Records, 48.
Plymouth Pilgrims, pastor, 48
Preachers, maintenance of, 54–56.
Presbyterian clergy, 69.
Presbyterians numerous in colonies, 61; Tiverton, 64.
Priests, 11; persecuting, 34; speculating, 37.
Privy Council, petition to and decision of, 58–70; mem-
bers present, 68.
Puritans, excesses, 33; aims, 58; rulers, 71; traditions,
72; cruelties apologized for, 73; bigotry, 80.
Pultney, William, 68.

QUAKER Baptists, 76.
Quaker Invasion of Massachusetts, 3, 41, 73–75.
Quakerism, fundamental principle, 15; outgrowth of
Puritanism, 36; notable converts, 47; opprobrious
epithets, 72, 73.
Quakers, origin of name, 6; arrival in Massachusetts,
42; hanged, 49; remonstrance, 51; scaffold, 72; fanat-
icism, 79; excesses, 80; relations to Indians, 83, 86–88.

Rayner's, Rev., brutality, 50.
Red Lyon Inn, law proclaimed, 45.
Resurrection of the body, 18.
Rhode Island, 48, 81, 87.
Richardson, Thomas, petition, 59–70.
Robinson, Isaac, 47.
Rogerines, 76.
Rogers, John, founder of a sect, 76.
Rothwell, anecdote, 55.

Saint Lawrence River, Indian question, 83.
Sale, Richard, 34.
Scudder, H. E., errors, 75.
Selden's *History*, 52.
Sisson, John, assessor, 58–70.
Southwick family, 81.
Spinning-wheel in church, 76.
Sprague's *Annals*, 48.
Stanyan, Temple, signature, 70.

Tabor, Philip, 58–70.
Taxes, 4, 51, 57–70, 89.
Testimonies, 26–28.
Theocracy in Massachusetts, 53.
Thee, in Quaker usage, 22.
Tithes, church, 22, 51, 52.
Titles, 23, 24.
Tiverton case, 57–70.
Truth and Innocency Defended, 77.

United Colonies, Indian troubles, 87.
Upsall, Dorothy, grave, 46.
Upsall, Nicholas, 45, 46.

Voice of God, 14. (See *Inward Light.*)
Voltaire on Penn's treaty, 82.

WALPOLE, SIR ROBERT, quoted, 78.

Wanton, Edward, signature, 57.

Weight of the meeting, 39.

Wharton family, influence for liberty, 81.

Whippings, public, 31, 44, 49, 50.

Whiting, John, book, 77, 78.

William and Mary, toleration, 8; charter, 59.

Williams, Roger, denounces the Quakers, 35, 36. (See *As to Roger Williams.*)

Winthrop, John, first resident governor, 48.

Winthrop, Samuel, Quaker, son of John, 48.

Women, right to preach, 26.

Worship, free, 60; Indian comment, 88.

YOUNG *Folks' History* cited, 51.

Your Excellency, and similar titles, 24.

Standard and Popular Library Books

SELECTED FROM THE CATALOGUE OF

HOUGHTON, MIFFLIN AND COMPANY.

A Club of One. An Anonymous Volume, $1.25.

Brooks Adams. The Emancipation of Massachusetts, crown 8vo, $1.50.

John Adams and Abigail Adams. Familiar Letters of, during the Revolution, 12mo, $2.00.

Oscar Fay Adams. Handbook of English Authors, 16mo, 75 cents ; Handbook of American Authors, 16mo, 75 cents.

Louis Agassiz. Methods of Study in Natural History, Illustrated, 12mo, $1.50; Geological Sketches, Series I. and II., 12mo, each, $1.50; A Journey in Brazil, Illustrated, 12mo, $2.50; Life and Letters, edited by his wife, 2 vols. 12mo, $4.00; Life and Works, 6 vols. $10.00.

Anne A. Agge and Mary M. Brooks. Marblehead Sketches. 4to, $3.00.

Elizabeth Akers. The Silver Bridge and other Poems, 16mo, $1.25.

Thomas Bailey Aldrich. Story of a Bad Boy, Illustrated, 12mo, $1.50; Marjorie Daw and Other People, 12mo, $1.50 ; Prudence Palfrey, 12mo, $1.50; The Queen of Sheba, 12mo, $1.50 ; The Stillwater Tragedy, 12mo, $1.50; Poems, *Household Edition*, Illustrated, 12mo, $1.75 ; full gilt, $2.25; The above six vols. 12mo, uniform, $9.00; From Ponkapog to Pesth, 16mo, $1.25 ; Poems, Complete, Illustrated, 8vo, $3.50 ; Mercedes, and Later Lyrics, cr. 8vo, $1.25.

Rev. A. V. G. Allen. Continuity of Christian Thought, 12mo, $2.00.

American Commonwealths. Per volume, 16mo, $1.25.
    Virginia. By John Esten Cooke.
    Oregon. By William Barrows.
    Maryland. By Wm. Hand Browne.
    Kentucky. By N. S. Shaler.
    Michigan. By Hon. T. M. Cooley.

Kansas. By Leverett W. Spring.
California. By Josiah Royce.
New York. By Ellis H. Roberts. 2 vols.
Connecticut. By Alexander Johnston.

(In Preparation.)

Tennessee. By James Phelan.
Pennsylvania. By Hon. Wayne MacVeagh.
Missouri. By Lucien Carr.
Ohio. By Rufus King.
New Jersey. By Austin Scott.

American Men of Letters. Per vol., with Portrait, 16mo, $1.25.

Washington Irving. By Charles Dudley Warner.
Noah Webster. By Horace E. Scudder.
Henry D. Thoreau. By Frank B. Sanborn.
George Ripley. By O. B. Frothingham.
J. Fenimore Cooper. By Prof. T. R. Lounsbury.
Margaret Fuller Ossoli. By T. W. Higginson.
Ralph Waldo Emerson. By Oliver Wendell Holmes.
Edgar Allan Poe. By George E. Woodberry.
Nathaniel Parker Willis. By H. A. Beers.

(In Preparation.)

Benjamin Franklin. By John Bach McMaster.
Nathaniel Hawthorne. By James Russell Lowell.
William Cullen Bryant. By John Bigelow.
Bayard Taylor. By J. R. G. Hassard.
William Gilmore Simms. By George W. Cable.

American Statesmen. Per vol., 16mo, $1.25.

John Quincy Adams. By John T. Morse, Jr.
Alexander Hamilton. By Henry Cabot Lodge.
John C. Calhoun. By Dr. H. von Holst.
Andrew Jackson. By Prof. W. G. Sumner.
John Randolph. By Henry Adams.
James Monroe. By Pres. D. C. Gilman.
Thomas Jefferson. By John T. Morse, Jr.
Daniel Webster. By Henry Cabot Lodge.
Albert Gallatin. By John Austin Stevens.
James Madison. By Sydney Howard Gay.
John Adams. By John T. Morse, Jr.

John Marshall. By Allan B. Magruder.
Samuel Adams. By J. K. Hosmer.
Thomas H. Benton. By Theodore Roosevelt.
Henry Clay. By Hon. Carl Schurz. 2 vols.

(*In Preparation.*)

Martin Van Buren. By Edward M. Shepard.
George Washington. By Henry Cabot Lodge. 2 vols.
Patrick Henry. By Moses Coit Tyler.

Martha Babcock Amory. Life of Copley, 8vo, $3.00.

Hans Christian Andersen. Complete Works, 10 vols. 12mo, each $1.00. New Edition, 10 vols. 12mo, $10.00.

Francis, Lord Bacon. Works, 15 vols. cr. 8vo, $33.75; *Popular Edition*, with Portraits, 2 vols. cr. 8vo, $5.00; Promus of Formularies and Elegancies, 8vo, $5.00; Life and Times of Bacon, 2 vols. cr. 8vo, $5.00.

L. H. Bailey, Jr. Talks Afield, Illustrated, 16mo, $1.00.

M. M. Ballou. Due West, cr. 8vo, $1.50; Due South, $1.50.

Henry A. Beers. The Thankless Muse. Poems. 16mo, $1.25.

E. D. R. Bianciardi. At Home in Italy, 16mo, $1.25.

William Henry Bishop. The House of a Merchant Prince, a Novel, 12mo, $1.50; Detmold, a Novel, 18mo, $1.25; Choy Susan and other Stories, 16mo, $1.25; The Golden Justice, 16mo, $1.25.

Bjornstjerne Bjornson. Complete Works. New Edition, 3 vols. 12mo, the set, $4.50; Synnove Solbakken, Bridal March, Captain Mansana, Magnhild, 16mo, each $1.00.

Anne C. Lynch Botta. Handbook of Universal Literature, New Edition, 12mo, $2.00.

British Poets. *Riverside Edition*, cr. 8vo, each $1.50; the set, 68 vols. $100.00.

Phillips Brooks. Oldest School in America. 16mo, $1.00.

John Brown, A. B. John Bunyan. Illustrated. 8vo, $4.50.

John Brown, M. D. Spare Hours, 3 vols. 16mo, each $1.50.

Robert Browning. Poems and Dramas, etc., 15 vols. 16mo, $22.00; Works, 8 vols. cr. 8vo, $13.00; Ferishtah's Fancies, cr. 8vo, $1.00; Jocoseria, 16mo, $1.00; cr. 8vo, $1.00; Parleyings with Certain People of Importance in their Day, 16mo or cr. 8vo, $1.25. Works, *New Edition*, 6 vols. cr. 8vo. $10.00.

William Cullen Bryant. Translation of Homer, The Iliad

cr. 8vo, $2.50 ; 2 vols. royal 8vo, $9.00 ; cr. 8vo, $4.00. The
Odyssey, cr. 8vo, $2.50 ; 2 vols. royal 8vo, $9.00 ; cr. 8vo, $4.00.

Sara C. Bull. Life of Ole Bull. *Popular Edition.* 12mo,
$1.50.

John Burroughs. Works, 7 vols. 16mo, each $1.50.

Thomas Carlyle. Essays, with Portrait and Index, 4 vols.
12mo, $7.50 ; *Popular Edition*, 2 vols. 12mo, $3.50.

Alice and Phœbe Cary. Poems, *Household Edition*, Illustrated, 12mo, $1.75 ; cr. 8vo, full gilt, $2.25 ; *Library Edition*,
including Memorial by Mary Clemmer, Portraits and 24 Illustrations, 8vo, $3.50.

Wm. Ellery Channing. Selections from His Note-Books,
$1.00.

Francis J. Child (Editor). English and Scottish Popular
Ballads. Eight Parts. (Parts I.–IV. now ready). 4to, each
$5.00. Poems of Religious Sorrow, Comfort, Counsel, and
Aspiration. 16mo, $1.25.

Lydia Maria Child. Looking Toward Sunset, 12mo, $2.50 ;
Letters, with Biography by Whittier, 16mo, $1.50.

James Freeman Clarke. Ten Great Religions, Parts I. and
II., 12mo, each $2.00 ; Common Sense in Religion, 12mo, $2.00 ;
Memorial and Biographical Sketches, 12mo, $2.00.

John Esten Cooke. My Lady Pokahontas, 16mo, $1.25.

James Fenimore Cooper. Works, new *Household Edition*,
Illustrated, 32 vols. 16mo, each $1.00 ; the set, $32.00 ; *Fireside Edition*, Illustrated, 16 vols. 12mo, $20.00.

Susan Fenimore Cooper. Rural Hours. 16mo, $1.25.

Charles Egbert Craddock. In the Tennessee Mountains,
16mo, $1.25 ; Down the Ravine, Illustrated, $1.00 ; The
Prophet of the Great Smoky Mountains, 16mo, $1.25 ; In The
Clouds, 16mo, $1.25.

C. P. Cranch. Ariel and Caliban. 16mo, $1.25 ; The Æneid
of Virgil. Translated by Cranch. 8vo. $2.50.

T. F. Crane. Italian Popular Tales, 8vo, $2.50.

F. Marion Crawford. To Leeward, 16mo, $1.25 ; A Roman
Singer, 16mo, $1.25 ; An American Politician, 16mo, $1.25.

M. Creighton. The Papacy during the Reformation, 4 vols.
8vo, $17.50.

Richard H. Dana. To Cuba and Back, 16mo, $1.25 ; Two
Years Before the Mast, 12mo, $1.00.

G. W. and Emma De Long. Voyage of the Jeannette. 2 vols. 8vo, $7.50; New One-Volume Edition, 8vo, $4.50.

Thomas De Quincey. Works, 12 vols. 12mo, each $1.50; the set, $18.00.

Madame De Stael. Germany, 12mo, $2.50.

Charles Dickens. Works, *Illustrated Library Edition*, with Dickens Dictionary, 30 vols. 12mo, each $1.50; the set, $45.00.

J. Lewis Diman. The Theistic Argument, etc., cr. 8vo, $2.00; Orations and Essays, cr. 8vo, $2.50.

Theodore A. Dodge. Patroclus and Penelope, Illustrated, 8vo, $3.00. The Same. Outline Illustrations. Cr. 8vo, $1.25.

E. P. Dole. Talks about Law. Cr. 8vo, $2.00; sheep, $2.50.

Eight Studies of the Lord's Day. 12mo, $1.50.

George Eliot. The Spanish Gypsy, a Poem, 16mo, $1.00.

Ralph Waldo Emerson. Works, *Riverside Edition*, 11 vols. each $1.75; the set, $19.25; *"Little Classic"* Edition, 11 vols. 18mo, each, $1.50; Parnassus, *Household Edition*, 12mo, $1.75; *Library Edition*, 8vo, $4.00; Poems, *Household Edition*, Portrait, 12mo, $1.75; Memoir, by J. Elliot Cabot, 2 vols. $3.50.

English Dramatists. Vols. 1–3, Marlowe's Works; Vols. 4–11, Middleton's Works; Vols. 12–14, Marston's Works; each vol. $3.00; *Large-Paper Edition*, each vol. $4.00.

Edgar Fawcett. A Hopeless Case, 18mo, $1.25; A Gentleman of Leisure, 18mo, $1.00; An Ambitious Woman, 12mo, $1.50.

Fénelon. Adventures of Telemachus, 12mo, $2.25.

James T. Fields. Yesterdays with Authors, 12mo, $2.00; 8vo, Illustrated, $3.00; Underbrush, 18mo, $1.25; Ballads and other Verses, 16mo, $1.00; The Family Library of British Poetry, royal 8vo, $5.00; Memoirs and Correspondence, cr. 8vo, $2.00.

John Fiske. Myths and Mythmakers, 12mo, $2.00; Outlines of Cosmic Philosophy, 2 vols. 8vo, $6.00; The Unseen World, and other Essays, 12mo, $2.00; Excursions of an Evolutionist, 12mo, $2.00; The Destiny of Man, 16mo, $1.00; The Idea of God, 16mo, $1.00; Darwinism, and Other Essays, New Edition, enlarged, 12mo, $2.00.

Edward Fitzgerald. Works. 2 vols. 8vo.

O. B. Frothingham. Life of W. H. Channing. Cr. 8vo, $2.00.

William H. Furness. Verses, 16mo, vellum, $1.25.

Gentleman's Magazine Library. 14 vols. 8vo, each $2.50;
Roxburgh, $3.50; *Large-Paper Edition*, $6.00. I. Manners and
Customs. II. Dialect, Proverbs, and Word-Lore. III. Pop-
ular Superstitions and Traditions. IV. English Traditions
and Foreign Customs. V., VI. Archæology. VII. Romano-
British Remains: Part I. (*Last two styles sold only in sets.*)

John F. Genung. Tennyson's In Memoriam, cr. 8vo, $1.25.

Johann Wolfgang von Goethe. Faust, Part First, Translated by C. T. Brooks, 16mo, $1.25; Faust, Translated by Bay-
ard Taylor, cr. 8vo, $2.50; 2 vols. royal 8vo, $9.00; 2 vols. 12mo,
$4.00; Correspondence with a Child, 12mo, $1.50; Wilhelm
Meister, Translated by Carlyle, 2 vols. 12mo, $3.00. Life, by
Lewes, together with the above five 12mo vols., the set, $9.00.

Oliver Goldsmith. The Vicar of Wakefield, 32mo, $1.00.

Charles George Gordon. Diaries and Letters, 8vo, $2.00.

George H. Gordon. Brook Farm to Cedar Mountain, 1861-2.
8vo, $3.00. Campaign of Army of Virginia, 1862. 8vo, $4.00.
A War Diary, 1863-5. 8vo, $3.00.

George Zabriskie Gray. The Children's Crusade, 12mo,
$1.50; Husband and Wife, 16mo, $1.00.

F. W. Gunsaulus. The Transfiguration of Christ. 16mo, $1.25.

Anna Davis Hallowell. James and Lucretia Mott, $2.00.

R. P. Hallowell. Quaker Invasion of Massachusetts, revised,
$1.25. The Pioneer Quakers, 16mo, $1.00.

Arthur Sherburne Hardy. But Yet a Woman, 16mo, $1.25;
The Wind of Destiny, 16mo, $1.25.

Bret Harte. Works, 6 vols. cr. 8vo, each $2.00; Poems,
Household Edition, Illustrated, 12mo, $1.75; cr. 8vo, full gilt,
$2.25; *Red-Line Edition*, small 4to, $2.50; *Cabinet Edition*,
$1.00; In the Carquinez Woods, 18mo, $1.00; Flip, and Found
at Blazing Star, 18mo, $1.00; On the Frontier, 18mo, $1.00;
By Shore and Sedge, 18mo, $1.00; Maruja, 18mo, $1.00;
Snow-Bound at Eagle's, 18mo, $1.00; The Queen of the Pirate
Isle, Illustrated, small 4to, $1.50; A Millionaire, etc., 18mo,
$1.00; The Crusade of the Excelsior, 16mo, $1.25.

Nathaniel Hawthorne. Works, *"Little Classic"* Edition,
Illustrated, 25 vols. 18mo, each $1.00; the set $25.00; *New
Riverside Edition*, Introductions by G. P. Lathrop, 11 Etchings and Portrait, 12 vols. cr. 8vo, each $2.00; *Wayside Edi-
tion*, with Introductions, Etchings, etc., 24 vols. 12mo, $36.00;

Fireside Edition, 6 vols. 12mo, $10.00; The Scarlet Letter, 12mo, $1.00.

John Hay. Pike County Ballads, 12mo, $1.50; Castilian Days, 16mo, $2.00.

Caroline Hazard. Memoir of J. L. Diman. Cr. 8vo, $2.00.

Franklin H. Head. Shakespeare's Insomnia. 16mo, parchment paper, 75 cents.

The Heart of the Weed. Anonymous Poems. 16mo, parchment paper, $1.00.

S. E. Herrick. Some Heretics of Yesterday. Cr. 8vo, $1.50.

George S. Hillard. Six Months in Italy. 12mo, $2.00.

Oliver Wendell Holmes. Poems, *Household Edition*, Illustrated, 12mo, $1.75; cr. 8vo, full gilt, $2.25; *Illustrated Library Edition*, 8vo, $3.50; *Handy-Volume Edition*, 2 vols. 32mo, $2.50; The Autocrat of the Breakfast-Table, cr. 8vo, $2.00; *Handy-Volume Edition*, 32mo, $1.25; The Professor at the Breakfast-Table, cr. 8vo, $2.00; The Poet at the Breakfast-Table, cr. 8vo, $2.00; Elsie Venner, cr. 8vo, $2.00; The Guardian Angel, cr. 8vo, $2.00; Medical Essays, cr. 8vo, $2.00; Pages from an Old Volume of Life, cr. 8vo, $2.00; John Lothrop Motley, A Memoir, 16mo, $1.50; Illustrated Poems, 8vo, $4.00; A Mortal Antipathy, cr. 8vo, $1.50; The Last Leaf, Illustrated, 4to, $10.00.

Nathaniel Holmes. The Authorship of Shakespeare. New Edition. 2 vols. $4.00.

Blanche Willis Howard. One Summer, Illustrated, 12mo, $1.25; One Year Abroad, 18mo, $1.25.

William D. Howells. Venetian Life, 12mo, $1.50; Italian Journeys, 12mo, $1.50; Their Wedding Journey, Illustrated, 12mo, $1.50; 18mo, $1.25; Suburban Sketches, Illustrated, 12mo, $1.50; A Chance Acquaintance, Illustrated, 12mo, $1.50; 18mo, $1.25; A Foregone Conclusion, 12mo, $1.50; The Lady of the Aroostook, 12mo, $1.50; The Undiscovered Country, 12mo, $1.50.

Thomas Hughes. Tom Brown's School-Days at Rugby, 16mo, $1.00; Tom Brown at Oxford, 16mo, $1.25; The Manliness of Christ, 16mo, $1.00; paper, 25 cents.

William Morris Hunt. Talks on Art, 2 Series, each $1.00.

Henry James. A Passionate Pilgrim and other Tales, 12mo, $2.00; Transatlantic Sketches, 12mo, $2.00; Roderick Hudson, 12mo, $2.00; The American, 12mo, $2.00; Watch and Ward, 18mo, $1.25; The Europeans, 12mo, $1.50; Confidence, 12mo, $1.50; The Portrait of a Lady, 12mo, $2.00.

Anna Jameson. Writings upon Art Subjects. New Edition, 10 vols. 16mo, the set, $12.50.

Sarah Orne Jewett. Deephaven, 18mo, $1.25; Old Friends and New, 18mo, $1.25; Country By-Ways, 18mo, $1.25; Play-Days, Stories for Children, square 16mo, $1.50; The Mate of the Daylight, 18mo, $1.25; A Country Doctor, 16mo, $1.25; A Marsh Island, 16mo, $1.25; A White Heron, 18mo, $1.25.

Rossiter Johnson. Little Classics, 18 vols. 18mo, each $1.00; the set, $18.00.

Samuel Johnson. Oriental Religions: India, 8vo, $5.00; China, 8vo, $5.00; Persia, 8vo, $5.00; Lectures, Essays, and Sermons, cr. 8vo, $1.75.

Charles C. Jones, Jr. History of Georgia, 2 vols. 8vo, $10.00.

Malcolm Kerr. The Far Interior. 2 vols. 8vo, $9.00.

Omar Khayyám. Rubáiyát, *Red-Line Edition*, square 16mo., $1.00; the same, with 56 Illustrations by Vedder, folio, $25.00; The Same, *Phototype Edition*, 4to, $12.50.

T. Starr King. Christianity and Humanity, with Portrait, 12mo, $1.50; Substance and Show, 16mo, $2.00.

Charles and Mary Lamb. Tales from Shakespeare. *Handy-Volume Edition.* 32mo, $1.00.

Henry Lansdell. Russian Central Asia. 2 vols. $10.00.

Lucy Larcom. Poems, 16mo, $1.25; An Idyl of Work, 16mo, $1.25; Wild Roses of Cape Ann and other Poems, 16mo, $1.25; Breathings of the Better Life, 18mo, $1.25; Poems, *Household Edition*, Illustrated, 12mo, $1.75; full gilt, $2.25; Beckonings for Every Day, 16mo, $1.00.

George Parsons Lathrop. A Study of Hawthorne 18mo, $1.25.

Henry C. Lea. Sacerdotal Celibacy, 8vo, $4.50.

Sophia and Harriet Lee. Canterbury Tales. New Edition. 3 vols. 12mo, $3.75.

Charles G. Leland. The Gypsies, cr. 8vo, $2.00; Algonquin Legends of New England, cr. 8vo, $2.00.

George Henry Lewes. The Story of Goethe's Life, Portrait, 12mo, $1.50; Problems of Life and Mind, 5 vols. 8vo, $14.00.

A. Parlett Lloyd. The Law of Divorce, cloth, $2.00; sheep, $2.50.

J. G. Lockhart. Life of Sir W. Scott, 3 vols. 12mo, $4.50.

Henry Cabot Lodge. Studies in History, cr. 8vo, $1.50.

Henry Wadsworth Longfellow. Complete Poetical and Prose Works, *Riverside Edition*, 11 vols. cr. 8vo, $16.50; Poetical Works, *Riverside Edition*, 6 vols. cr. 8vo, $9.00; *Cambridge Edition*, 4 vols. 12mo, $7.00; Poems, *Octavo Edition*, Portrait and 300 Illustrations, $7.50; *Household Edition*, Illustrated, 12mo, $1.75; cr. 8vo, full gilt, $2.25; *Red-Line Edition*, Portrait and 12 Illustrations, small 4to, $2.50; *Cabinet Edition*, $1.00; *Library Edition*, Portrait and 32 Illustrations, 8vo, $3.50; Christus, *Household Edition*, $1.75; cr. 8vo, full gilt, $2.25; *Cabinet Edition*, $1.00; Prose Works, *Riverside Edition*, 2 vols. cr. 8vo, $3.00; Hyperion, 16mo, $1.50; Kavanagh, 16mo, $1.50; Outre-Mer, 16mo, $1.50; In the Harbor, 16mo, $1.00; Michael Angelo: a Drama, Illustrated, folio, $5.00; Twenty Poems, Illustrated, small 4to, $2.50; Translation of the Divina Commedia of Dante, *Riverside Edition*, 3 vols. cr. 8vo, $4.50; 1 vol. cr. 8vo, $2.50; 3 vols. royal 8vo, $13.50; cr. 8vo, $4.50; Poets and Poetry of Europe, royal 8vo, $5.00; Poems of Places, 31 vols. each $1.00; the set, $25.00.

James Russell Lowell. Poems, *Red-Line Edition*, Portrait, Illustrated, small 4to, $2.50; *Household Edition*, Illustrated, 12mo, $1.75; cr. 8vo, full gilt, $2.25; *Library Edition*, Portrait and 32 Illustrations, 8vo, $3.50; *Cabinet Edition*, $1.00; Fireside Travels, 12mo, $1.50; Among my Books, Series I. and II. 12mo, each $2.00; My Study Windows, 12mo, $2.00; Democracy and other Addresses, 16mo, $1.25; Uncollected Poems.

Thomas Babington Macaulay. Works, 16 vols. 12mo, $20.00.

Mrs. Madison. Memoirs and Letters of Dolly Madison, 16mo, $1.25.

Harriet Martineau. Autobiography, New Edition, 2 vols. 12mo, $4.00; Household Education, 18mo, $1.25.

H. B. McClellan. The Life and Campaigns of Maj.-Gen. J. E. B. Stuart. With Portrait and Maps, 8vo, $3.00.

G. W. Melville. In the Lena Delta, Maps and Illustrations, 8vo, $2.50.

T. C. Mendenhall. A Century of Electricity. 16mo, $1.25.

Owen Meredith. Poems, *Household Edition*, Illustrated, 12mo, $1.75; cr. 8vo, full gilt, $2.25; *Library Edition*, Portrait and 32 Illustrations, 8vo, $3.50; Lucile, *Red-Line Edition*, 8 Illustrations, small 4to, $2.50; *Cabinet Edition*, 8 Illustrations, $1.00.

Olive Thorne Miller. Bird-Ways, 16mo, $1.25.

John Milton. Paradise Lost. *Handy-Volume Edition.* 32mo, $1.00. *Riverside Classic Edition*, 16mo, Illustrated, $1.00.

S. Weir Mitchell. In War Time, 16mo, $1.25; Roland Blake, 16mo, $1.25.

J. W. Mollett. Illustrated Dictionary of Words used in Art and Archæology, small 4to, $5.00.

Montaigne. Complete Works, Portrait, 4 vols. 12mo, $7.50.

William Mountford. Euthanasy, 12mo, $2.00.

T. Mozley. Reminiscences of Oriel College, etc., 2 vols. 16mo, $3.00.

Elisha Mulford. The Nation, 8vo, $2.50; The Republic of God, 8vo, $2.00.

T. T. Munger. On the Threshold, 16mo, $1.00; The Freedom of Faith, 16mo, $1.50; Lamps and Paths, 16mo, $1.00; The Appeal to Life, 16mo, $1.50.

J. A. W. Neander. History of the Christian Religion and Church, with Index volume, 6 vols. 8vo, $20.00; Index, $3.00.

Joseph Neilson. Memories of Rufus Choate, 8vo, $5.00.

Charles Eliot Norton. Notes of Travel in Italy, 16mo, $1.25; Translation of Dante's New Life, royal 8vo, $3.00.

Wm. D. O'Connor. Hamlet's Note-Book, 16mo, $1.00.

G. H. Palmer. Trans. of Homer's Odyssey, 1–12, 8vo, $2.50.

Leighton Parks. His Star in the East. Cr. 8vo, $1.50.

James Parton. Life of Benjamin Franklin, 2 vols. 8vo, $5.00; Life of Thomas Jefferson, 8vo, $2.50; Life of Aaron Burr, 2 vols. 8vo, $5.00; Life of Andrew Jackson, 3 vols. 8vo, $7.50; Life of Horace Greeley, 8vo, $2.50; General Butler in New Orleans, 8vo, $2.50; Humorous Poetry of the English Language, 12mo, $1.75; full gilt, $2.25; Famous Americans of Recent Times, 8vo, $2.50; Life of Voltaire, 2 vols. 8vo, $6.00; The French Parnassus, 12mo, $1.75; crown 8vo, $3.50; Captains of Industry, 16mo, $1.25.

Blaise Pascal. Thoughts, 12mo, $2.25; Letters, 12mo, $2.25.

Elizabeth Stuart Phelps. The Gates Ajar, 16mo, $1.50; Beyond the Gates, 16mo, $1.25; Men, Women, and Ghosts, 16mo, $1.50; Hedged In, 16mo, $1.50; The Silent Partner, 16mo, $1.50; The Story of Avis, 16mo, $1.50; Sealed Orders, and other Stories, 16mo, $1.50; Friends: A Duet, 16mo, $1.25; Doctor Zay, 16mo, $1.25; Songs of the Silent World, 16mo, gilt top, $1.25; An Old Maid's Paradise, 16mo, paper, 50 cents; Burglars in Paradise, 16mo, paper, 50 cents; Madonna of the Tubs, cr. 8vo, Illustrated, $1.50.

Phillips Exeter Lectures: Delivered before the Students of Phillips Exeter Academy, 1885-6. By E. E. HALE, PHILLIPS BROOKS, Presidents MCCOSH, PORTER, and others. 12mo, $1.50.

Mrs. S. M. B. Piatt. Selected Poems, 16mo, $1.50.

Carl Ploetz. Epitome of Universal History, 12mo, $3.00.

Antonin Lefevre Pontalis. The Life of John DeWitt, Grand Pensionary of Holland, 2 vols. 8vo, $9.00.

Margaret J. Preston. Colonial Ballads, 16mo, $1.25.

Adelaide A. Procter. Poems, *Cabinet Edition*, $1.00; *Red-Line Edition*, small 4to, $2.50.

Progressive Orthodoxy. 16mo, $1.00.

Sampson Reed. Growth of the Mind, 16mo, $1.00.

C. F. Richardson. Primer of American Literature, 18mo, $.30.

Riverside Aldine Series. Each volume, 16mo, $1.00. First edition, $1.50. 1. Marjorie Daw, etc., by T. B. ALDRICH; 2. My Summer in a Garden, by C. D. WARNER; 3. Fireside Travels, by J. R. LOWELL; 4. The Luck of Roaring Camp, etc., by BRET HARTE; 5, 6. Venetian Life, 2 vols., by W. D. HOWELLS; 7. Wake Robin, by JOHN BURROUGHS; 8, 9. The Biglow Papers, 2 vols., by J. R. LOWELL; 10. Backlog Studies, by C. D. WARNER.

Henry Crabb Robinson. Diary, Reminiscences, etc. cr. 8vo, $2.50.

John C. Ropes. The First Napoleon, with Maps, cr. 8vo, $2.00.

Josiah Royce. Religious Aspect of Philosophy, 12mo, $2.00.

Edgar Evertson Saltus. Balzac, cr. 8vo, $1.25; The Philosophy of Disenchantment, cr. 8vo, $1.25.

John Godfrey Saxe. Poems, *Red-Line Edition*, Illustrated, small 4to, $2.50; *Cabinet Edition*, $1.00; *Household Edition*, Illustrated, 12mo, $1.75; full gilt, cr. 8vo, $2.25.

Sir Walter Scott. Waverley Novels, *Illustrated Library Edition*, 25 vols. 12mo, each $1.00; the set, $25.00; Tales of a Grandfather, 3 vols. 12mo, $4.50; Poems, *Red-Line Edition* Illustrated, small 4to, $2.50; *Cabinet Edition*, $1.00.

W. H. Seward. Works, 5 vols. 8vo, $15.00; Diplomatic History of the War, 8vo, $3.00.

John Campbell Shairp. Culture and Religion, 16mo, $1.25; Poetic Interpretation of Nature, 16mo, $1.25; Studies in Poetry and Philosophy, 16mo, $1.50; Aspects of Poetry, 16mo, $1.50.

William Shakespeare. Works, edited by R. G. White, *Riverside Edition*, 3 vols. cr. 8vo, $7.50; The Same, 6 vols., cr. 8vo, uncut, $10.00; The Blackfriars Shakespeare, per vol. $2.50, *net.* (*In Press.*)

A. P. Sinnett. Esoteric Buddhism, 16mo, $1.25; The Occult World, 16mo, $1.25.

M. C. D. Silsbee. A Half Century in Salem. 16mo.

Dr. William Smith. Bible Dictionary, *American Edition*, 4 vols. 8vo, $20.00.

Edmund Clarence Stedman. Poems, *Farringford Edition*, Portrait, 16mo, $2.00; *Household Edition*, Illustrated, 12mo, $1.75; full gilt, cr. 8vo, $2.25; Victorian Poets, 12mo, $2.00; Poets of America, 12mo, $2.25. The set, 3 vols., uniform, 12mo, $6.00; Edgar Allan Poe, an Essay, vellum, 18mo, $1.00.

W. W. Story. Poems, 2 vols. 16mo, $2.50; Fiammetta: A Novel, 16mo, $1.25. Roba di Roma, 2 vols. 16mo.

Harriet Beecher Stowe. Novels and Stories, 10 vols. 12mo, uniform, each $1.50; A Dog's Mission, Little Pussy Willow, Queer Little People, Illustrated, small 4to, each $1.25; Uncle Tom's Cabin, 100 Illustrations, 8vo, $3.00; *Library Edition*, Illustrated, 12mo, $2.00; *Popular Edition*, 12mo, $1.00.

Jonathan Swift. Works, *Edition de Luxe*, 19 vols. 8vo, the set, $76.00.

T. P. Taswell-Langmead. English Constitutional History. New Edition, revised, 8vo, $7.50.

Bayard Taylor. Poetical Works, *Household Edition*, 12mo, $1.75; cr. 8vo, full gilt, $2.25; Melodies of Verse, 18mo, vellum, $1.00; Life and Letters, 2 vols. 12mo, $4.00; Dramatic Poems, 12mo, $2.25; *Household Edition*, 12mo, $1.75; Life and Poetical Works, 6 vols. uniform. Including Life, 2 vols.; Faust, 2 vols.; Poems, 1 vol.; Dramatic Poems, 1 vol. The set, cr. 8vo, $12.00.

Alfred Tennyson. Poems, *Household Edition*, Portrait and Illustrations, 12mo, $1.75; full gilt, cr. 8vo, $2.25; *Illustrated Crown Edition*, 2 vols. 8vo, $5.00; *Library Edition*, Portrait and 60 Illustrations, 8vo, $3.50; *Red-Line Edition*, Portrait and Illustrations, small 4to, $2.50; *Cabinet Edition*, $1.00; Complete Works, *Riverside Edition*, 6 vols. cr. 8vo, $6.00.

Celia Thaxter. Among the Isles of Shoals, 18mo, $1.25; Poems, small 4to, $1.50; Drift-Weed, 18mo, $1.50; Poems for Children, Illustrated, small 4to, $1.50; Cruise of the Mystery, Poems, 16mo, $1.00.

Edith M. Thomas. A New Year's Masque and other Poems, 16mo, $1.50; The Round Year, 16mo, $1.25.

Joseph P. Thompson. American Comments on European Questions, 8vo, $3.00.

Henry D. Thoreau. Works, 9 vols. 12mo, each $1.50; the set, $13.50.

George Ticknor. History of Spanish Literature, 3 vols. 8vo, $10.00; Life, Letters, and Journals, Portraits, 2 vols. 12mo, $4.00.

Bradford Torrey. Birds in the Bush, 16mo, $1.25.

Sophus Tromholt. Under the Rays of the Aurora Borealis, Illustrated, 2 vols. $7.50.

Mrs. Schuyler Van Rensselaer. H. H. Richardson and his Works.

Jones Very. Essays and Poems, cr. 8vo, $2.00.

Annie Wall. Story of Sordello, told in Prose, 16mo, $1.00.

Charles Dudley Warner. My Summer in a Garden, *Riverside Aldine Edition*, 16mo, $1.00; *Illustrated Edition*, square 16mo, $1.50; Saunterings, 18mo, $1.25; Backlog Studies, Illustrated, square 16mo, $1.50; *Riverside Aldine Edition*, 16mo, $1.00; Baddeck, and that Sort of Thing, 18mo, $1.00; My Winter on the Nile, cr. 8vo, $2.00; In the Levant, cr. 8vo, $2.00; Being a Boy, Illustrated, square 16mo, $1.50; In the

Wilderness, 18mo, 75 cents; A Roundabout Journey, 12mo, $1.50.

William F. Warren, LL. D.   Paradise Found, cr. 8vo, $2.00.

William A. Wheeler.   Dictionary of Noted Names of Fiction, 12mo, $2.00.

Edwin P. Whipple.   Essays, 6 vols. cr. 8vo, each $1.50.

Richard Grant White.   Every-Day English, 12mo, $2.00; Words and their Uses, 12mo, $2.00; England Without and Within, 12mo, $2.00; The Fate of Mansfield Humphreys, 16mo, $1.25; Studies in Shakespeare, 12mo, $1.75.

Mrs. A. D. T. Whitney.   Stories, 12 vols. 12mo, each $1.50; Mother Goose for Grown Folks, 12mo, $1.50; Pansies, 16mo, $1.25; Daffodils, 16mo, $1.25; Just How, 16mo, $1.00; Bonnyborough, 12mo, $1.50; Holy Tides, 16mo, 75 cents; Homespun Yarns, 12mo, $1.50.

John Greenleaf Whittier.   Poems, *Household Edition*, Illustrated, 12mo, $1.75; full gilt, cr. 8vo, $2.25; *Cambridge Edition*, Portrait, 3 vols. 12mo, $5.25; *Red-Line Edition*, Portrait, Illustrated, small 4to, $2.50; *Cabinet Edition*, $1.00; *Library Edition*, Portrait, 32 Illustrations, 8vo, $3.50; Prose Works, *Cambridge Edition*, 2 vols. 12mo, $3.50; The Bay of Seven Islands, Portrait, 16mo, $1.00; John Woolman's Journal, Introduction by Whittier, $1.50; Child Life in Poetry, selected by Whittier, Illustrated, 12mo, $2.00; Child Life in Prose, 12mo, $2.00; Songs of Three Centuries, selected by Whittier: *Household Edition*, Illustrated, 12mo, $1.75; full gilt, cr. 8vo, $2.25; *Library Edition*, 32 Illustrations, 8vo, $3.50; Text and Verse, 18mo, 75 cents; Poems of Nature, 4to, Illustrated, $6.00; St. Gregory's Guest, etc., 16mo, vellum, $1.00.

Woodrow Wilson.   Congressional Government, 16mo, $1.25.

J. A. Wilstach.   Translation of Virgil's Works, 2 vols. cr. 8vo, $5.00.

Justin Winsor.   Reader's Handbook of American Revolution, 16mo, $1.25.

W. B. Wright.   Ancient Cities from the Dawn to the Daylight, 16mo, $1.25.